STACEY ESPINO

EVERNIGHT PUBLISHING ®

www.evernightpublishing.com

ROUGH AND READY

STACEY ESPINO

And suddenly you know: It's time to start something new and trust the magic of beginnings.

— Meister Eckhart

STACEY ESPINO

ROUGH AND READY

Heels and Spurs, 1

Stacey Espino

Copyright © 2018

Chapter One

Robyn snorted, nearly choking on her martini. "Stop!"

"*What?*"

Shelly, her friend and co-worker, gave her a look of mock innocence. They'd been talking about men, sex, and everything in between. When an older couple gave them a hard look after Shelly said the word "cock" a little too loudly, Robyn couldn't keep from laughing. The situation was as hilarious as her own sex life, or lack thereof. She was thirty-seven and had never dated a man worth keeping. They all seemed so superficial, but after two decades of failed relationships, she started to wonder if maybe she was the problem.

The older couple moved out of ear shot. "Anyway, as we were saying, I think size does matter," said Robyn.

"So you don't believe it's *how they use it*?" Shelly snickered, picking at the mixed nuts at their table.

"To a degree, I guess."

"Well, you can't make that kind of statement

unless you can back it up," she said. "Have you had a really big co—"

Robyn pressed a finger to her friend's lips. "Oh no, you don't. If you forget, we work with most of the people in here."

Metrosexual was always bustling on Friday nights. Being dead center in the business district, it was a quick escape for suits after a long week at the office.

"Fine, then answer the question."

She shrugged. "I don't know. Maybe." In truth, she wasn't too sure. Her friends believed she was more experienced in the bedroom than she actually was. And she'd never really had an orgasm-worthy encounter. Maybe she was meeting all the wrong men.

Shelly finished off her third drink. "Robyn, you can tell by their hands and feet. *Really.* Haven't you heard the old adage? The bigger the boots, the bigger the—"

"Got it!" she snapped, looking to both sides. "But maybe it's more than size or how they use it. I mean, I'm not getting any younger. I think I might need more than sex from a man."

Shelly frowned. "Put that thought out of your head if you want to keep sane. Trust me, there's no such thing as a happily ever after. Not in this life, and certainly not in this damn city."

"I guess." She swirled her drink around the glass, watching the liquid move like lazy waves, suddenly feeling very, very sorry for herself.

"You need to get laid before we head to Hicksville next week. You'll drive me nuts on the trip. Fairy tale sickness never did anyone any good."

"What's that, exactly?" asked Robyn, almost afraid of the answer.

"I know your type. You think every guy you meet

is *the one*, your soul mate, different from all the others. In reality, they're all the same. Price Charming doesn't exist."

Robyn forced a smile. In her circle of friends, life was a thrill-ride, a fast-paced adventure with no time for inner reflection. Beauty, status, and money were everything. They were paralegals at a hectic legal practice. As long as she didn't stay quiet for too long, she never had the chance to realize how shitty her personal life actually was. Maybe it was for the best. She had to stay high on life in order to avoid it.

On Monday, they had to travel north to farm country to deal with land disputes involving a proposed oil pipeline. Big money was involved, so Robyn had little choice but to agree to her boss Calloway's assignment. She was used to life in the courtroom, lunch downtown, and drinks with friends by night. Leaving her comfort zone to spend a week or more in questionable motel rooms wasn't her idea of a good time. In fact, the idea of sleeping in a strange bed made her anxiety levels shoot through the roof. At least she was partnered with Shelly, so she wouldn't suffer alone.

"Remember Trey from accounting?" asked Shelly. "He was sweet as pie until I spent the night with him. Now he can't even look me in the eye."

"He's a pig. You should have known better." Trey was a notorious office playboy. Robyn had nearly succumbed to his flirting herself.

Shelly attempted to get the olive out of her glass with a finger. "Of course I knew better, but I fucked him anyway. You've seen him. Whatever, that was just an example to prove my point. Men can't be trusted."

They sat quietly at their window seats for the next twenty minutes or so, watching people walk by from behind the tinted glass. Her friend would occasionally offer strict fashion commentary. Many passersby were loving couples, which only made her feel more miserable about her situation.

Robyn absently studied the glow of the streetlights against the darkness of the evening, insects clamoring for position, and the familiar ache started deep in her gut. The emptiness continually ate away at her, leaving her little more than a shell of a woman. She'd conformed, tried to fit in, but it all meant nothing in the grand scheme of things. She craved authenticity, love, something worth living for beyond the almighty dollar.

Robyn checked her watch, an expensive knockoff Tudor. "I've gotta get home. I have a lot to get done before we head out Monday. What car we taking?"

"My SUV. Calloway's reimbursing me for gas and mileage. I'll pick you up at your place around three."

It was a long drive to her apartment east of the city. The suburbs were the only place to find reasonable rent. She parked underground and rode up to the eighth floor. The elevator smelled like urine.

Once inside her apartment, she kicked off her heels and tossed her purse. She flicked on the table lamp and powered up her laptop—the usual drill. There were thirty new messages. She sat down, the soft glow of the computer illuminating the kitchen table. As she suspected, most were responses from the profile she'd added to a free dating site. She clicked open one message and immediately deleted it when she saw the pic of an elderly man in a Speedo.

Fuck this shit.

She was an educated woman. Surely she knew Mr. Right wouldn't be waiting on a cheap dating site. Then why did she keep looking? Robyn ground her teeth together and shut the lid of her computer with exaggerated force. She'd have to settle for her battery-operated boyfriend. He was always eager to please. If only *he* could stave off the loneliness. Shelly was right. No real man would ever measure up to her hopes and desires. And the cold-hard fact really sucked.

Robyn unzipped her skirt and shapewear girdle as she headed to her bedroom. She looked at her figure in the full-length mirror, shifting her hips from side to side in the flattering shadows. If only she had more time to hit the gym. Apparently she had a little too much in all the right places. The girls at work said she needed to get work done—it was the norm for their circles, expected even. She wasn't so sure she should take that permanent leap in an attempt to achieve perfection.

What was it about being alone at night that brought out all her insecurities? Without all the hustle and bustle, just her thoughts, it was debilitating.

She looked down to the darkened streets below. The quiet was deafening. There had to be more to life than this. She'd missed the train, failed to settle down with a husband and have children at her prime. Now she just existed, coasting through life with no purpose. Loneliness devastated her at every opportunity. She noticed those extra white hairs and new wrinkles frequently cropping up. Who the fuck would want her now? She sighed and climbed into bed, deciding she needed to get a prescription ASAP, anything to get her through the evening hours. Did they bottle hope? Was there a cure for being pathetic? Maybe she just needed to get a cat.

****

Her bags were packed and ready by Monday morning. The dishes and laundry were done, assignments completed, clients contacted, and she'd gotten her nails and hair done yesterday afternoon. The morning light always gave her new optimism, the previous night's desperation mercifully forgotten. She was ready to raise some hell in the backwoods with Shelly. She hoped they'd finalize things quickly and be back in the city much sooner than expected.

The lobby bell sounded right on time, and Robyn buzzed her friend in. She touched up her lipstick in the foyer mirror, unlocked the door, and then checked around the apartment to ensure all the lights were off. When she heard a male voice coming from the living room, her breath caught. She hadn't even made sure it was Shelly buzzing. *Idiot.*

She cautiously peeked around the corner from her bedroom, wondering what she'd use as a weapon, if necessary. Her pepper spray was inconveniently in her purse by the front door. Her body sank in relief when she saw Shelly with the stranger. But who the hell was he?

"Hey," she said as she entered the room, smoothing her hands down her hips to straighten her fitted jacket. Robyn tried to appear unfazed, even though her heart was still racing.

"Change of plans. Sort of," said Shelly. "Calloway's sending back-up." Her friend winked.

"Good morning. Peter Brighton…" The man attempted to offer a hand, but Shelly reached for his forearm.

"He's one of Calloway's top guys, top of his class, too."

Top of anything he wants. The guy was tall and lean, clean-cut, and had a swagger that screamed old money. This was the kind of man she needed to sweep her off her feet. She discretely took in the lines of his designer suit and the cute dimple that appeared when he smiled.

"So it'll be the three of us?" Robyn asked.

Shelly picked up the small suitcase Robyn had set

by the door and started to head out. "Three's company, right?"

After locking up, she caught up with Peter and Shelly by the elevators. It was a bit awkward with the strange guy in tow, and she imagined countless hours in the car together would either be torture or the start of something wonderful. With a high profile lawyer as her boyfriend, she wouldn't have to worry for anything. He'd love and take care of her, make the world and its worries disappear.

Ha, who am I kidding?

Once in the elevator, she noticed Peter grimace from the smell. She was utterly humiliated that he knew this was where she lived. He was probably used to the very best, some waterfront condo downtown. Why did Shelly have to bring him upstairs with her?

"We're meeting a contact at a restaurant called Meg's Longhorn," said Shelly, readjusting Robyn's suitcase strap on her shoulder. She didn't bother asking for it back because she knew Shelly would refuse.

"A steakhouse," said Peter with sudden interest. "In three hours we'll be ready for a proper meal."

Food was the last thing on her mind. Part of her resented the fact she was stuck on this road trip, but another part anxiously hoped for something more— adventure, romance, purpose. Maybe she was teamed up with Peter for a reason. Or maybe she really did have fairy tale sickness.

When they reached Shelly's SUV, conveniently parked in the no-parking zone, she wondered who should take the passenger seat. Peter had major rank on her, but Shelly was also her close friend. Robyn took slow, measured steps so she wouldn't be put in the position of choosing her seat first.

Shelly placed Robyn's bag in the back beside a

few others and then headed to the driver's seat. When Peter opened the rear passenger door, she thought he was about to go in. Instead, he held it open for her to enter. She quickly climbed in and was surprised when Peter took the seat next to her, leaving Shelly alone in the front. It was the last thing she expected.

"Cozy?" he asked, that dimple making its appearance again.

"*Very.*"

This was getting more interesting by the second. A lawyer, with everything going for him, was actually showing interest. Was her luck in love finally changing?

After starting the car, Shelly scowled at her from the rear view mirror, but kept her mouth shut, which was unusual for her. Did her friend have dibs on Peter? Shelly never mentioned him before, but she did live moment-to-moment most days. Robyn decided to keep the flirting to a minimum until she had a chance to talk with her friend in private. It was going to be one long, uncomfortable trip.

Chapter Two

Yukon winced after dropping his weight on the first available diner stool. Every muscle ached, and all he could think about was sleep. His leather boot creaked as he rested his foot on the bar rail.

"Coffee?"

He nodded to Marcy, the regular waitress at the Longhorn. The scent of back bacon and chili reminded him he hadn't eaten since lunch. And he was too tired to give a shit. It was eight o'clock at night, and he would have still been working if the setting sun hadn't cut him short.

"You look like shit," said Gage. The faint scent of tobacco marked his friend's arrival.

Yukon didn't even turn to the side, rather focused on the grease stains and callouses on his fingers. He was frustrated beyond measure after the fucked-up day he'd had. "The tractor's gone to shit."

"I told you last year it was on its last leg," said Gage. He sat on the stool next to him, dropping his keys and a pack of smokes on the counter. "You're stubborn as a mule."

His ground his teeth but couldn't keep quiet. "Stubborn has nothing to do with it. If I had the damned money, I'd get it fixed right or lease a new one." His attention was diverted when Marcy set down his coffee. He took a cleansing breath. "Anyway, tomorrow's another day, right?"

"The Palmer brothers have three new machines. They'll harvest your fields—"

"For a hefty price," Yukon interrupted. "We're lucky to put food on the table these days. Same as everyone else."

Most families in their farming community were hurting after the harsh season they'd had. A too-long winter followed by a dry summer had hurt crops. While prices were high on the market due to the shortages, farmers didn't see a dime of it. Now, on top of a meager crop, his only decent tractor decided to fail him when he needed it most.

He took a sip of his black coffee.

"I'd help if I could. Fuck, you know that, don't you?" asked Gage.

Yukon couldn't stand pity. His friend was a cattle farmer a few ranches over. They'd traded manure for feed corn for generations. But Gage couldn't control the weather or change Yukon's bad luck.

Days like today he almost wished he could swap harvesting for shoveling cow shit.

"I know." He reached into his back pocket for his wallet and pulled out two dollars. He slapped them on the counter before standing. Tonight he'd make for bad company, and he didn't want to piss off a good friend. He'd head home and get as much sleep as he could before starting over again at five in the morning.

Marcy leaned over the counter before he had a chance to leave. "Ya'll hear about Ms. Granger?" When neither of them answered, she continued. "Apparently she's been going without. Mack stopped by and found out she hadn't had a proper meal for days."

Fuck.

"Well ain't that just bullshit," said Gage. "Why didn't she say anything?"

Marcy only shrugged before heading off to help another customer. She didn't need to explain because the answer was always the same. *Pride.* Their community may be hard hit, but its people were unbreakable and often pig headed—himself included.

He left the diner feeling worse off than when he'd entered. Sometimes life just wasn't fair—the rich getting richer, the poor suffering needlessly. The cowbell clanged against the glass as the door closed behind him. The crisp evening air was a welcome relief after suffering under the sun all day. There'd been talk of a storm moving their way, but he doubted they'd see rain any time soon. He walked along the gravel drive to his pick-up truck, his thoughts pulled in too many directions.

It was only a five-minute drive to his ranch. He needed sleep in the worst way. Each bump in the road jostled him enough to keep him from falling asleep at the wheel. He pulled into the driveway. The flood lights on the barns were off, so he grabbed a flashlight out of the glove box before getting out of the truck. It was quiet, too quiet. Sometimes the lull of country living could drive a man to insanity. Only his footsteps against the brittle grass cut the deafening silence. He vaguely remembered a time when he savored the quiet nights, but his memories of the past were a blur.

He prayed for sleep, but knew it was unlikely he'd get much tonight. Yukon worried about Ms. Granger, suffering in silence only two minutes away. He'd make sure to head over first thing in the morning to see her needs were met. A cowboy couldn't call himself a man if he ignored a widow in need, or any neighbor for that matter.

He opened the side door to the house and flicked on the light. The first thing he noticed was his brother passed out on the couch. He hadn't even made it to his room. The scent of cheap whiskey hung in the air. Some nights Yukon wished he had an escape like alcohol, but turning into a drunk wasn't the miracle cure to his troubles. He knew from experience that Parker only made his headaches worse by indulging himself.

Yukon tossed his Stetson onto the coffee table and then turned to the fridge. The interior was as empty as it had been this morning. He'd have to take a few side jobs in between fiddling with his tractor. At this point, the ancient machine was only held together by blood, sweat, and salvaged parts. If his father was still around, he'd have the thing running like new in no time. Yukon should have paid better attention when he'd had the chance.

"Hey…" His older brother leaned up on one elbow and attempted to find something in the front pocket of his flannel shirt. "Buy food tomorrow." He tossed a rolled wad of money on the coffee table and then dropped back down.

Yukon closed the fridge, frowning from the archway of the kitchen. He walked over to the couch and eased off his brother's cowboy boots, one at a time, before sitting in the armchair across from him. "Should I even ask where that came from?"

Parker draped his forearm across his eyes, effectively ignoring him.

"Ms. Granger's been going hungry." He reached for the roll of money and examined it, wondering what the fuck Parker had done to get it.

"Get her taken care of," Parker said dismissively.

Yukon headed up the stairs to the second level of the house. Each step was punctuated with a creak in the wood. He was tempted to be an asshole and yell at his brother to be up at dawn to help him fix the tractor, but decided to keep his mouth shut. Even though he didn't like the secrets between them, he was thankful for the money. They lived a simple life, but they couldn't survive on air and water alone.

He took a cold shower before bed, allowing the stress of the day to wash away. As he brushed his teeth, he studied the old scars on his shoulders and chest. His body was hard and weathered. He wasn't a boy anymore—he was a grown man and not getting any younger. Where the fuck had the time gone? Lines were evident at the corners of his eyes and his new stubble was thick and coarse. He was becoming his father. Would he die alone in the same way, bitter and regretful? When had things gone wrong?

Despite his worries, his body needed to recharge. Yukon crashed onto his bed, the heavy patchwork quilt cushioning his fall. He briefly stared at the cracks in the ceiling before closing his eyes.

He hoped his brother was still home come morning.

****

He'd slept in. Yukon cursed as he rushed out of bed and danced into his jeans. The bright sunlight beaming through the cracks of the curtains was testament to the day passing him by. He bolted down the stairs two at a time while buttoning up his plaid shirt.

Parker was still sleeping on the sofa, which somehow pleased Yukon. At least it meant he was alive and out of trouble. His brother was the only family he had left in this world. He grabbed his keys off the counter and squinted as he opened the heavy wooden door. The sun was bright, not a cloud in the sky. It felt good against his skin, but would soon become a curse if the mercury kept rising like it had yesterday.

After boarding his pick-up truck, he began piecing together his day. First, he had to head to the market to get food for Ms. Granger, then get parts for his tractor with the money Parker gave him. He'd spend a couple hours working on the piece of shit. It wouldn't stop there because he also needed to get a side job—the roll of cash would only sustain them so long. As much as he hated the thought, he might have to ask the Palmer brothers for work. He knew they had a need for seasoned herders this time of year, but also knew the best they'd offer him was mucking out stalls or worse. The rivalry between their two families had been raging on since he was in grade school. He'd made a pact with Parker to never sink low enough to ask them for work, but times were tough and Yukon had a difficult decision to make.

He found a parking spot on the periphery of the open market. Two of his friends, Mack and Carlson, were just leaving.

"Hey, Yukon!"

Yukon opened the tailgate of Mack's truck so he could unload the bag of grain on his shoulder. "Slacking off, I see."

"Don't worry about me, big boy," said Mack. "I've been working my ass off since sunrise."

Yukon ran a hand through his hair. "I just woke up."

"Must be nice," said Carlson. "You retired now?"

"Maybe when I'm ninety, and even then, I'll probably be sweating out in the fields."

Mack leaned against his truck and lit up a cigarette. "We've got to head back to work. Gage is dropping off our vaccines at lunch, so we have to coral the first run."

His friends worked for one of the larger cattle operations just north of town. It seemed the majority of farmers were opting to raise cattle over fickle cash crops. Yukon and Parker didn't have the start-up capital to make the switch, so they had to keep on keepin' on.

Yukon pulled out his wad of cash. "I'm visiting Ms. Granger. Then I'm off to the junk yard to look for parts."

"Here." Mack took a twenty dollar bill out of his

wallet. Carlson did the same. Word about Ms. Granger had likely spread like wildfire. Yukon knew his friends were hurting for money the same as him, but they all looked out for each other in their community. Every one of them had been on the receiving end at some point. Their little town had his heart and always would.

Yukon took the money and added it to his pocket. He'd give the extra cash to Ms. Granger when he drove over with the food. Bartering was used more often than money, and he knew the older woman would offer him preserves or a hand-knit tea cozy when he showed up. He'd take whatever she offered, knowing it would keep her dignity intact. He still had a few memories of his mother. She was the first one to teach him about charity and the importance of ensuring it was done with mindful tact. He missed his parents.

The market was always quiet weekday mornings, especially Mondays. A roll of tumbleweed lazily rolled across the near-empty lot as if to prove his point. "Will you be at the Longhorn's tonight?" he asked.

His friends boarded the truck, slamming the doors shut almost simultaneously. "After what today's promising to be, hell yes." Mack tipped his Stetson while balancing a cigarette between two fingers. As he backed the truck out, the midday sun reflected off the chrome surfaces, making Yukon squint.

Carlson leaned out the open passenger window. "Oh yeah, how's Parker healing up?"

He frowned, not having a clue what Carlson was talking about. "Good, I guess, he's home sleeping."

Yukon clenched his jaw hard enough to ache. He wondered what the fuck his brother had done this time. He had promised not to ride in the rodeo events after nearly killing himself two summers ago at the Calgary Stampede. But what did Yukon expect? How else could

Parker have earned the cash so fast?

He'd definitely have to crawl to the Palmer brothers for work. He wouldn't watch his brother risk life and limb just to provide for them. There were always better ways.

As he walked along the well-beaten paths between fruit and vegetable stands, he heard arguing behind one of the small outbuildings. His first thought was tourists. They'd been passing through in hordes the past week to get to one of the large rodeos about fifty miles up north. They never stayed long enough to be a benefit to their local economy. The only evidence was their litter and drunken episodes when they'd stop by at night. He couldn't wait until their roads were safe and quiet once again.

"Don't touch me," the female voice called out.

One of the old women pointed to the outbuilding when he looked her way, no doubt knowing he'd intervene. Knowing any man in their community would do the right thing.

When he turned the corner, he wasn't expecting to find the Palmers' younger sister, Amy, at the mercy of a man he'd never seen. She worked part-time at the market during the summers. And she was only eighteen, just a girl.

Without thought or hesitation, Yukon tugged the man away by the shoulder. "There a problem here?"

The man had a light beard and scowled with intent when he made eye contact. "She's trying to rip me off!"

A small group of local women began to gather on the periphery, the men off working the farms. Amy shook her head, her eyes heavy with unshed tears. "He gave me a ten and said it was a twenty when I gave him the change. I don't even have a twenty."

"He put his hands on you?"

"You're not her father, so fuck off," interrupted the stranger. He braced his arm against the outbuilding, too close to Amy's head.

Yukon wasn't in the mood to deal with this asshole. He had shit to get done and a million things on his mind.

He nodded for Amy to leave. "Go, get out of here." When the man attempted to grab her arm, Yukon moved quickly. He cupped his hand at the man's throat and slammed him up against the wooden boards. The entire structure shook.

"You're not welcome here, stranger. I suggest you make haste getting the fuck out of our town." He added pressure to the man's neck until his cheeks flushed red. But as soon as he released him and stepped back, the bastard threw a cheap shot, clocking Yukon right in the jaw. Before he could plan his next move, he was struck with something on the back of the head, making his vision swim. There were two of them. He attempted to shake it off, using a hand on the outbuilding for support.

Yukon could hear the muffled sound of women screaming. He had to get his shit together fast. This wasn't the first brawl he'd been in and likely wouldn't be the last.

"Not so tough now, are you, country boy?"

He didn't answer. Yukon barreled forward, taking the guy down to the ground with him in a billow of dust. He didn't need all his faculties to fight dirty, just his muscles. And he had no short supply. They rolled around the dusty ground, striking and struggling. Pain wasn't even an afterthought, only coming out on top. He could smell the stench of alcohol on the man. His vision began to clear as they fought, his second wind giving him the energy to dominate. He straddled the man, delivering blow after blow, releasing his anger and frustration.

A shotgun fired, ringing his ears.

Gage stood over them, gun casually resting on his shoulder. He was shaking his head in mock irritation, shadows blocking his expression.

Yukon rolled off the man, leaning up on his elbows. "Why're *you* at the market? I thought you were doing an inoculation."

He shrugged. "Rose flagged down my truck. You're lucky I was passing by."

"Hey, I had things handled."

"Sure, Yukon."

When the guy he'd been fighting started to sit up, Gage used the barrel of his gun to motion exactly where he wanted him to go. The two men didn't say a word as they rushed off to their car.

"Next time it won't be a warning shot!" Gage called out. He reached a hand down and helped yank Yukon to his feet.

The crowd dispersed, life returning back to normal. He bent down to pick up his Stetson, using it to brush the dust off his jeans. The piece of two-by-four lying on the ground by his boots reminded him his head ached and face hurt. And he still hadn't accomplished anything on his to-do list.

"Okay then, I'll see you tonight at the diner?"

Yukon clapped his friend on the shoulder. "Tonight I'll be having something stronger than coffee."

Chapter Three

"Are you sure we're in the right place?" asked Peter.

After driving for five hours, getting lost three times, and growing closer to starvation by the minute, they passed a sign signaling they were approaching their destination. The only problem—they were literally in the middle of nowhere. There was nothing but open fields in every direction, no sign of a five-star hotel or steakhouse. Why would Calloway send one of his best lawyers and two paralegals into the boondocks?

"That's what the GPS says," said Shelly from the front seat.

Robyn knew her friend was on her last nerve. From fighting traffic getting out of the city to the multiple near misses with wild animals, including a stubborn cow, she was definitely in a less-than-stellar mood.

"There's something up ahead," said Robyn, pointing. It wasn't much, but she could see the outline of multiple buildings in the near distance. She hoped it wasn't just another run-down ranch. Shelly was right, this was Hicksville in its finest, and Robyn couldn't wait to get back to civilization.

"It better fucking be!" Shelly hit the accelerator and clouds of dust billowed out from behind the SUV. She'd stopped putting on appearances for Peter hours ago.

Peter leaned into her space to look out the window on her side of the SUV. He made a disgusted grumble after taking in the endless wheat fields. "Calloway owes me one," he said. "You must be hungry?"

"I think I forgot about my hunger an hour ago," Robyn half joked. In truth, the whole trip made her uneasy. She wasn't good with changes in her routine. That one-bedroom apartment on the outskirts of the city might not be much, but it was her safe haven. And even though her nights were lonely, at least she had a place to call home. Her hardened exterior started in childhood, grew tenfold on the job, and was solidified by high societal expectations. It wasn't easy being a woman trying to move up the corporate ladder.

"Oh thank God, I think this might actually be it," said Shelly as they neared the buildings. It appeared to be a drive-thru town with no structure over two stories high. Robyn knew they were coming to farming country, but not this far off the grid.

"Let's just find this Longhorn Steakhouse before the sun sets. I don't see any streetlights out here." Peter appeared more uneasy than she felt. And if he was expecting upscale dining, she had a feeling he'd be sorely disappointed.

Shelly parked the SUV and they all got out, looking around like they'd landed on the surface of Mars. Her friend pointed at the wooden building just ahead. The mangled sign read *Meg's Longhorn*, but it wasn't a restaurant. On its best day it could be called a truck stop. She felt dirty looking at it.

Peter shifted his briefcase from one hand to the other. He looked like a fish out of water, his eyes narrowed as if insulted just standing in this so-called town. "What's the contact's name?" he asked. "I've never wanted to get documents signed faster than today."

"Marla Winters." Shelly read from a piece of paper as she stepped up onto the wooden plank walkway. "But we were supposed to be here hours ago. I doubt she's waiting."

Robyn followed along, careful not to get her stilettos stuck in the cracks on the walkway. The air was dry and hot, with the scent of fresh-cut hay. With the sun low on the horizon, night wasn't far off. Her skirt suit made it difficult to walk, but she found her sexuality an asset in the courtroom. Since they were meeting a woman, it would probably work against her. At least she was getting points with Peter—she hoped. He was everything she'd ever wanted, if only she could convince him she was worthy of his attention. It seemed she'd been trying to prove herself in one way or another since she could walk.

If Shelly gave her the green light, she'd do everything in her power to get in Peter's good graces.

As Peter pushed open the door, old-fashioned bells clanged against the glass. The diner had a few mountain men at the counter in dusty plaid shirts. There were also some people eating at one of the far tables. It smelled like bacon grease. As she walked, her heels clicked on the tiles, garnering them the full attention of everyone in the diner.

"Can I help you?" asked a middle-aged waitress from behind the counter. She looked like she'd smoked all her life, her skin coarse and weathered.

"Yes, we were supposed to meet a woman here a few hours ago. Would you happen to know a Ms. Winters?" asked Shelly, tossing her perfectly coiffed blonde curl behind her shoulder.

The woman shrugged. "There was some lady in a suit here earlier. She had a coffee, read the paper, then left."

"Do you know where she lives?"

"Honey, I wouldn't know that. I can tell you she wasn't from around here."

Robyn looked around the room. Many tiles on the

floor were cracked, the grout filthy. Just about everything was in some state of disrepair—from the tables and chairs to the blinds and ceiling fans. A small, out-of-date television playing sports sat high behind the cash register. The guys at the end of the counter stared at her. Her skin crawled.

Shelly turned to Peter. "I have a contact number. Does your phone get any reception out here? Mine doesn't."

Peter pulled a new iPhone out of his breast pocket, every move smooth and unrushed. "Only one bar."

"What are we going to do?" Robyn whispered. They couldn't just sit around and do nothing. The sun was starting to set, a streak of pink already making its appearance beyond the windows. Where would they sleep? What would they eat?

"We'll have to call Ms. Winters and have her come back," said Peter. He turned around to face the counter again. "Excuse me, do you have a public phone we could use?"

"Sorry, no phone."

"Of course not," he muttered, turning back around.

"Let's talk in the truck," said Shelly.

They left the diner and gathered outside the SUV. "Look, this isn't what I signed up for," said Peter. "This place would never pass a health inspection in the city, and I have a court case to prepare for. One of us should wait here, while the others drive until they get reception. We need to get this Marla woman to come back to the diner so I can sign off on this deal."

Robyn was more confused than ever. From what she understood, they were supposed to work out a deal that could take at least a few days. Peter made this sound like it would last two minutes—if they could get in touch with their contact.

"I'll drive south until I get reception," said Shelly. "You two can wait here and get a bite to eat."

Robyn could hear the hint of resentment in her friend's voice. She grabbed Shelly's arm and dragged her a few feet off. "Can I talk to you for a second?"

"What?"

They moved away from the SUV. "Did I do something to piss you off? I didn't ask Peter to sit beside me, Shelly. That's the problem, isn't it?"

Shelly subtly rolled her eyes. "It doesn't matter. We're not in high school, Robyn. He obviously likes you, so it's fine. I'll get the next one."

"Forget it, I'll wait here. Take him with you for the drive. He's not even my type."

"Bullshit."

Robyn groaned. "He's a pretty boy—definitely your type."

"You sure?"

"Of course, I'm sure. Rock his world," she teased. "Just don't come crying to me if he forgets your name tomorrow morning like Trey."

"*Shut up.*" Shelly couldn't wipe the smile off her face.

After sorting out a few details, Shelly and Peter took off in the SUV in search of cell phone reception. She supposed they'd make the perfect couple, both inhumanly beautiful and refined. Shelly had had three elective surgeries in the last two years, and she planned for more. Perfection, it seemed, was an addiction. Robyn had to wait at the diner for the contact in case Shelly was able to reach her. She hadn't really thought of the consequences of offering to stay in the town alone. All that had mattered at the time was preserving her friendship with Shelly, even if it cost her a potential relationship with any paralegal's wet dream. Now she had to go back into that creepy little diner. Alone.

Robyn decided to waste as much time as possible outside. If she had any luck, they'd be back in a few minutes. She looked for a clean spot on the wooden walkway and sat down. The warm breeze made the dust on the road swirl like mini cyclones. She lost herself in thought.

Every time she lifted her eyes to the sky, it seemed to have grown darker. She made patterns in the dirt with her heels, her mind drifting. Why couldn't her life be easier? Most of the women she associated with had it all, while she struggled just to keep up to par. It wasn't fair. The odds had been stacked against her from an early age, and no matter how hard she worked, or how hard she tried to be accepted, it was never enough. Sure, she'd molded her image and put on a good front, but that was all it was. Sitting here in the middle of nowhere, the evening chill creeping in with the darkness, made her realize how lost she truly was.

Her stomach growled.

She began to think they'd forgotten about her, and desperation started creeping in. The sun had been replaced by more stars than she'd ever seen in her life. If she wasn't so terrified, it would have been beautiful. When she heard the rumble of a vehicle and saw bouncing headlights approaching, she almost laughed out loud with relief.

It wasn't a rescue. Two trucks raced by, leaving her in a cloud of dust and exhaust. Another came soon after, braking in front of the diner with only inches to spare. Four men got out of the pick-up truck. They were rowdy and obnoxious, and she was thankful they didn't notice her sitting by herself in the dark. Walking the downtown city streets as night didn't feel nearly as daunting as her current situation.

She checked her watch, thankful for the glowing hands. Shelly and Peter had been gone five minutes short of two hours, and she had to pee. Her phone was dead and she'd lost all hope, that familiar sense of abandonment blackening her thoughts. How could Shelly just forget about her? It was impossibly dark beyond the glow of the diner, the drone of crickets deafening. What was she supposed to do with herself? She had no way of communicating with anyone and no vehicle. She also couldn't decide if it was safer to stay where she was on the edge of darkness or brave the jerks in the diner. If things got ugly, there wasn't even a public phone to rely on. Were there even cops way out here in nowhere land? How long would it take them to show up if there was a problem?

Her mind whirled.

When Robyn felt herself crumbling apart, her defenses took over. She had to keep strong. Her next decision was made when she heard coyotes crying in the near distance. She bolted to her feet and trotted to the entrance of the diner. Her heart raced just imagining all those creepy drunken eyes on her, but she had little choice. There was nowhere else to go in this micro town.

She took a deep breath and pushed open the door, those damn bells announcing her entrance. Luckily for her, the raucous patrons and loud game playing on the television drowned out the sound. The atmosphere had changed since she'd first entered.

Robyn approached the empty end of the counter, trying to appear invisible.

"You're back," said the waitress. "You find who you were looking for?"

"No, actually." What else was she supposed to

say? Her friends abandoned her in this backwards town? "Is there a restroom here?"

"Sure. Around the corner, honey." She motioned to the right. "Can I get any food started for you?"

That was when Robyn realized her purse was in the backseat of the SUV. *Fuck me!* Her face must have blanched because the waitress suddenly started doting, setting a glass of water in front of her. She focused on her breathing. Surely Shelly would come back at some point. Maybe they had car trouble. Or maybe they'd shacked up at a five-star in the city. It wouldn't be unlike her friend to put a one-night stand above their friendship. Robyn seemed to come in second for everyone in her life.

She escaped into the bathroom. The tiny unisex room had two stalls and one sink. It was in worse disrepair than the actual diner, piss stains galore, but right now that was her last concern. She turned on the tap and splashed water on her face. Robyn studied her image in the mirror. *I look like shit. Worse than shit.* She looked tired and drawn out, her perfectly styled hair now flat and lacking any luster. Forget touching up her make-up, because all her supplies were in her purse. It was much harder to keep up appearances now than when she was in her twenties.

Her mind kept creating different escape scenarios, anything to get her out of this nightmare. She kept coming up empty. Without a working phone, money, or a ride—she was royally screwed.

Chapter Four

Yukon drove by his neighbor's ranch, stopping on the road to see if Gage was finished for the night. He could see shadowy figures clamoring near the trucks, thanks to the powerful flood lights. The cattle had been corralled, so he knew his friend would be joining him for a few drinks.

His day had been extraordinary, and not in a good way. At least he'd set out and accomplished everything on his list. He touched the back of his head, some of his hair still encrusted with blood from the morning fight at the market. His cheek felt sore and swollen, too. Once he got home, he'd shower away the day and let time take care of his wounds.

A truck traveled up the long, dark drive, stopping once alongside his. "Ready for trouble?" asked Gage.

He leaned out his window. "Ready as I'll ever be for a Monday."

"Mack and Carlson are gonna meet up with us later at the Longhorn."

Yukon put the truck into "drive." He should have been heading home to sleep. And he needed to stop pretending everything was fine and have a serious talk with Parker. If they kept going down the same road, they'd be strangers before long.

The diner was only minutes away, doubling as the town bar by night. He turned to face the fields after slamming his door shut, pulling on his padded jacket. Pitch blackness blanketed the land, the tiny town the only light in the vast farming country. This community was his heart.

The rumble of Gage's pick-up grew louder as it neared, the headlights bobbing up and down along the old dirt road.

He leaned against his tailgate as he waited. A few drinks with the guys was just what the doctor ordered. But he'd be lying to himself if he said this was the life he'd imagined for himself. A lot of the men he'd grown up with had families to go home to at the end of a long day. It would be nice to have someone waiting for him. The love of a good woman was more valuable than gold in these parts. Yukon wasn't getting any younger, so even a family would soon be out of reach.

"How'd the repairs go?" asked Gage.

"It's working. I'll be testing it out first thing in the morning."

"About time. I'm up to my ears in manure. I need it gone."

They entered the diner together. The bright light and numerous voices were a welcome distraction from Yukon's dismal thoughts. It was best to keep his mind busy so it didn't have a chance to wander.

Gage nudged him in the ribs, bringing his attention to the group of outsiders busy drinking in the far corner. They liked to think of the Longhorn as their local hangout, not a tourist destination.

Yukon sat on a free stool, running a hand through his hair to keep it off his face. "Who're our friends, Marcy?"

"Assholes would be a compliment," she said. "I'm sure they'll make a fuss when they realize I've cut them off."

"Don't worry. We'll be here for a while," said Gage.

She started setting out two white coffee mugs, but Yukon shook his head. "My day was too fucked up for coffee, darlin'."

Marcy smiled and reached under the counter for

the shot glasses.

"I haven't seen Parker in a while. Where's he at?" she asked.

"He's one of the things I'm trying to forget."

She filled the glasses with mind-numbing whiskey, giving him a wink before heading down the counter.

"How's he healing up anyway?" asked Gage.

"Why does everyone know what Parker's up to except me? I'm the one living with him." He downed his shot and tapped the counter for another.

"Hey, I just saw him getting bound up at the doctors when I stopped by for my prescription. I don't know any details. Didn't even talk with him."

"I imagine he's riding bulls again. With the rodeo so close this year, it only makes sense."

Gage shrugged off his overcoat and tossed it on the empty stool next to him. "You should have gotten yourself checked out today, but I'm guessing you didn't."

Yukon rubbed his face, his stubble already coming in thick. The blow hadn't knocked him out, just stole his senses for a spell. "I'll live."

"If you say so."

His attention was diverted to movement at the far end of the bar. "Who's that?"

Marcy was back filling up their glasses. "Can't say for sure. Definitely not from around these parts."

The woman in question approached the counter from the bathroom. Her dark hair fell in soft waves over her shoulders. She was dressed in a body-hugging skirt suit, her legs going on forever. She was fucking perfect. And definitely not local.

"Holy shit," Gage mumbled after spinning to face the woman.

"Hey, I saw her first."

They both stared as she walked to the opposite end of the counter. Every step she took had him focusing on those lush curves. There weren't many available women in their town. They were either married, close friends, or nothing to rouse his interest. This woman made his cock firm up without effort. She attempted to wiggle up onto a stool but her skirt was too tight. It was amusing watching her struggle. What was a city girl doing way out here?

Yukon decided she was waiting for her boyfriend. Not smart of him to leave her alone at this hour. Or in this shithole.

"Marcy, send her a drink. Tell her it's from me," said Yukon.

"You paying for that drink?"

He'd known Marcy all his life, but he still narrowed his eyes as if insulted.

"Okay fine, but I don't expect she'll be interested in the likes of either one of you."

"Just give her the drink. Something fancy."

Marcy walked over to the lone woman at the end of the counter, setting an open bottle of beer in front of her. The cute thing scowled at the offering and then turned to look at them with a look of pure evil. *Fuck.*

Gage laughed out loud and clapped him on the shoulder. "Sorry about that, buddy. The bad luck day must want to hang on 'til midnight."

So much for getting lucky.

****

Robyn brushed the bottle of beer to the side. Her stomach was already complaining because she'd gone too long without eating. The smell of the alcohol under her nose nearly pushed her over the edge. When the waitress said the drink was from the hillbilly down the counter, she wanted to crawl into a hole and die. They were probably toothless with beer bellies and body odor strong enough to make her gag. The bigger one even had a black eye for God's sake. She needed to get the fuck out of Dodge.

The crash of a wooden chair falling to the ground made Robyn jump. Several men stood up in the far corner, swearing and shouting. The bar suddenly felt way too small.

"I have the fucking money, so give me what I ordered!"

"Sorry, it's time to go home, boys," said the waitress. She looked so small and helpless with the group of drunken men around her, but she held her ground. Adrenaline flooded Robyn's veins. What would happen if one of those jerks tried to hurt the waitress? Who would help her?

She planned to kill Shelly for this.

"Are you the law?" shouted another man. He stumbled back, grabbing his friend for balance.

Just when Robyn thought things were about to get completely out of control, the hillbilly and his friend casually slipped off their stools and moved toward the commotion. They didn't appear as fazed as she felt, rather inconvenienced.

Once they approached the chaos, the drunks shifted their focus away from the waitress. Robyn exhaled in relief, deciding the distraction was a good time to get out of the bar. She'd be safer braving the coyotes than staying another minute in this redneck paradise. As she attempted to slip out unnoticed, a man was shoved into her. Her high heels didn't offer much balance and she nearly toppled over—into the arms of another man.

"Well, hello, sunshine." A couple more cowboys

entered the diner, looking at her like she was fresh meat. She was surrounded. Robyn shrugged him off, walking backward as she felt for the door handle.

A beer bottle smashed, making her yelp.

"You're scaring her, Carlson," the hillbilly called out. "And keep your hands to yourself. She's mine."

Carlson chuckled, a deep rumbling sound. He brushed by her, unfazed, moving to the heart of the melee with the other newcomer. She turned around briefly before reaching for the door. There was a regular bar fight going down, fists flying, and bodies colliding. She wrenched open the door and rushed out into the cool night air, free at last. Robyn rested against the side of the building, leaning over her knees to catch her wits. This was bullshit. If she were home, she'd be climbing into her lush bedding about now. She barely had time to sort her thoughts when the door flew open and a body crashed onto the walkway with a loud thud. The other troublemakers were shoved outside, all swearing and protesting.

Robyn tiptoed away, desperate to stay hidden from sight. She pressed her back flat against the far end of the building, hoping the darkness and wooden support columns would conceal her. If Shelly showed up right now, she'd be so relieved to be rescued that she wouldn't even complain about being left behind. Well, not at first. *Please show up, please show up...*

The men boarded their truck and sprayed gravel as they peeled off down the road into the darkness. Quiet returned to the night. She closed her eyes and exhaled, willing herself to stay calm and collected.

"You lost?"

Robyn's heart jolted back to life as she opened her eyes and looked *up, up, up*. The hillbilly with the black eye was right in front of her. He was shadowed, only the light from the diner's windows and door highlighting his frame, but she knew it was him. She refused to look him in the eyes, unwilling to antagonize the beast. How had he found her? Why hadn't she heard his footsteps?

"Cat got your tongue?"

She bit the inside of her lip. How would she get out of this mess? Was he going to rape her? Chop her up and feed her to his pigs?

When he reached out and tilted her head up with a bent finger, the contact startled her. She attempted to bolt back, but she was already pinned against the building.

"I'm not the one you have to worry about, so no need to be skittish. What's your name, darlin'?"

"R–Robyn."

"I've never seen you around. You just passing through?"

She relaxed a degree. The calm tone of his voice was almost soothing after the night she'd had. "I'm waiting for someone."

"Boyfriend?"

Robyn shook her head. "Business partners." She rubbed her arms to stave off the chill.

"You shouldn't be waiting outside. I promise there'll be no more trouble inside tonight."

She didn't know what to do at this point. Then those hellhounds started howling again, singing to the moon.

Robyn gasped.

"Don't you worry about them either," he said.

How could he sound so confident? It was even enough to give her a false sense of security.

"Do you have a cell phone?"

His chuckle was a deep, all-encompassing sound.

"Sorry. Don't have one of those."

He stepped back, tilted his hat, and began to walk away. She reluctantly followed him back to the entrance. *Who doesn't own a cell phone?* The rowdy drunks had been scared off, so she supposed it was safer inside than it had been. She still wanted to be anywhere else.

Robyn slipped inside as he held open the door, rushing to her distant spot at the bar. She felt safer near the waitress, the only other female in the place.

When she turned to the side, he was sitting on a stool beside her, his three friends looking on from the other end of the counter.

"It's getting late. You sure your *business partners* are going to show up?" His tone fueled the anger deep-seated in her gut—the anger ignited by Shelly's abandonment, and her miserable predicament.

"I'm very sure." She wouldn't even bet on her chances at this point, but she felt the need to hide any weakness from this stranger.

"My name's Yukon, by the way. You hungry? Thirsty?"

This time she turned her head enough to really take in the hillbilly for the first time. She was surprised when he didn't match the horrific image she'd created in her mind's eye. He was ruggedly handsome with piercingly blue eyes and dark shaggy hair. The five o'clock shadow was heavy across his jaw, and what she thought was a black eye was actually a bruised cheek.

In fact, his friends weren't homely mountain men either, but appealing cowboys, tall and strong. Her dire predicament suddenly took an equally uncomfortable turn. She wasn't attracted to working-class men. They were rough, dirty, and no-holds-barred—completely uncivilized. She couldn't stand small towns or the people who lived in them. What she wanted was a man like

Peter, a refined man with style and class. The fact her body was taking notice of Yukon, cataloging every masculine detail, was unacceptable.

"I don't have my purse."

He smirked. "That's not what I asked you."

Back home, Robyn took care of herself. She worked hard to portray herself as a confident, modern woman because appearances were everything. But for some reason, it wasn't as easy to put on a front with Yukon. He made her feel feminine and submissive—all her insecurities open for inspection.

"Last call!" the waitress yelled. A collective groan resounded throughout the diner. She turned the television off, the sudden quiet making Robyn shudder. *Shit!* What would she do now? Her only safe haven was about to close for the night. If she was going to wake up from a nightmare, it needed to be soon.

She'd been so busy sorting her worried thoughts that she'd forgotten about the man beside her. When she turned slightly to see if he was still waiting for her to answer, he was staring. Why did he have to have such fuck-me eyes? And why was she thinking about sex when she had much more serious things to worry about? Her traitorous body was trying to unravel her.

Chapter Five

Yukon was striking out at every turn. The city girl wanted nothing to do with him, but he had no plans on giving up just yet. For the first time in weeks, he was thinking about something other than sleep or his shitty life. His problems came second to his new attraction for the little brunette. He felt at least ten years younger, ready to take on the world.

"Come on, let's get rolling," said Carlson.

His friends stood, paid their tabs, and began to head to the door. He needed more time.

"You need a ride somewhere?" he asked.

She shook her head, not looking directly at him. Maybe she did hate him. Gage would never let him forget this night.

He grabbed his Stetson off the counter, at a complete loss for words. "You have a nice evening, ma'am."

Yukon joined his friends outside the diner, fighting the urge to turn back. There'd been something there, some spark when she looked him in the eyes. She was just too stubborn for her own damn good.

"How'd it go?" Mack lit up a cigarette, taking a deep drag. "She gonna warm your bed tonight?"

He could hear the poorly contained chuckles of amusement from his friends.

"Fuck off," he grumbled, walking away from the light of the diner. "I never asked her to come home with me."

"Does that mean she's up for grabs?"

He opened the door to his truck. Before climbing in, he turned. "Don't even dream it, Mack. I told you she's mine."

Yukon drove home in a half daze. He didn't even remember how tired, pissed, or sore he was. All he could think about were those haunting eyes and killer curves. He kicked off his boots after slamming the side door of the house shut.

Parker came down the stairs with a towel wrapped around his waist, his hair still damp. "You make enough noise to wake the dead." He froze before adding, "What the fuck happened to your face?"

He ignored his brother, too happy to argue or deal with any of the pending drama.

"You get the fields plowed?" Parker asked.

Yukon crashed on the threadbare sofa. "Didn't you see for yourself?"

"I got in late."

"Again? You have another job I don't know about? Because as far as I know money doesn't grow on trees."

"I didn't see you complain when you took the cash yesterday." Parker grabbed a beer before taking the chair, a mismatched piece with paisley print.

"You know what, never mind. I don't want to deal with anything tonight that can ruin my good mood."

Parker cocked an eyebrow. "What the fuck are you grinning about?"

He shrugged. "I met the woman I'm gonna marry."

His brother nearly choked on his beer. "Is that so?" He chuckled. "Who is it? Sally from the feed store? Bailey from the hog ranch?"

Parker purposely mentioned women he couldn't stand. It was nice to see him smile, though. It reminded him of simpler days when they were still young and optimistic. When they hadn't turned into strangers.

"A city girl. Gorgeous little thing."

"And she likes *you*?"

"She does. She just doesn't know it yet."

Parker laughed again, reclining in the chair to rest his feet up on the couch. "Where's she at now, little brother? Waiting for you in your dreams?"

"*Cute*. I imagine she's staying with Kate for the night. I'll try and prove myself to her first thing tomorrow."

Now Parker took notice, sitting up straighter, his beer hanging in a loose fist between his legs. "For real? What on earth would a city girl want with this god-forsaken place? And why you?"

Yukon scowled. "Someone left her behind at the diner without a ride. She wouldn't give me the time of day, even when Marcy started shutting down for the night."

"That where you got the shiner?"

"No, but I'm sure she considered it."

Parker nodded, easing back into the chair. "What she look like?"

He shrugged. "You'd love her, no doubt—long hair, curves in all the right places, and evil eyes. I never knew a woman in a suit could look that damn fine." Just thinking about the brunette made his cock harden.

"I like evil."

There was a knock at the door, startling them both. They didn't get many visitors, especially at this hour. Yukon's immediate thought was there had to be trouble, maybe with Ms. Granger or another neighbor. Bad news seemed to come when he least expected it. He rose to his feet and didn't hesitate to wrench open the door. If it turned out to be unwelcome company, he could handle himself. And his shotgun and rifle were always within reach.

"Sorry, honey, but she's your problem now. I

have to be up at four and Momma needs her beauty sleep." Marcy began to walk away, revealing a very bewildered-looking city girl. He couldn't believe Robyn was standing in his doorway.

"Speak of the devil…"

He turned and glared at Parker to shut him up. Yukon needed to figure out what the fuck was happening, and he needed to remember how to speak in a hurry.

"She brought me to the boarding house but the owner wasn't there."

"Kate's place."

"What?"

"The owner, her name's Kate. She's the owner of the boarding house." He felt like an oversized idiot, and knew Parker likely thought the same thing.

"The phone lines are down. I asked the waitress if I could stay with her for one night, but—"

"Yeah, Marcy's real particular about houseguests." Marcy was an icon in their little town, a mother figure to many of the cowboys, including him some days. She wasn't sugar and spice, and rarely asked anyone for help, even when she had to deal with assholes at the diner. Although she'd give you the shirt off her back, she never let a soul inside her little trailer behind the diner.

"I don't know what else to do. I'm sorry she brought me here…"

He suddenly realized Robyn was still standing in the doorway, the cold night air swirling around her bare legs. Did she actually think she was unwelcome?

"No, she did right. Come inside. Please." He held his arm out, inviting her to enter. She hesitated, only taking one step inside before stopping. "It ain't pretty but it's warm and we have an extra bed upstairs."

Why wasn't she coming inside? He knew their old house was simplistic and hadn't been remodeled—ever, but it was a good, solid home. Maybe she was used to something luxurious and modern. They were more about functionality rather than fancy décor. Maybe what he had to offer would never be enough.

"You're scaring her, Yukon." Parker leaned against the kitchen wall, still nursing a beer. He looked her up and down with interest. A hint of amusement played on his features.

"Scared?" He turned back to Robyn, now noticing the uncertainty in her eyes. His older brother had more experience than him in most areas, especially women.

"Look at her," said Parker. "She's as nervous as a fawn in the headlights."

****

Parker didn't think much about his brother's sudden infatuation until he saw the woman in the flesh. She had an hourglass figure, full hips, and a maiden-in-distress quality that piqued his interest. And he wasn't attracted to educated women. City slickers were a headache he barely tolerated. There'd be some at the annual rodeo events, plenty at the dude ranches he used to work during the summer, and they'd even pass through their little town—like now.

But this one ... this one whet his appetite, one he thought he had better control of. She was cute, despite her refined clothes and salon hair. A woman like her would eat Yukon alive. His brother was used to homegrown cowgirls and farmer's daughters, not businesswomen ready to trade their soul for a paycheck.

"I don't know you," she said to Yukon. "Or him."

She sought reassurance. He'd seen it more times than he could count, but usually from much younger women.

Parker smiled, stepping closer to the entryway. "I'm his brother, baby girl. And I don't know how men behave in the city, but around here they don't take from a woman that's not giving."

"That's not what I meant," she stammered.

"Then why so nervous?"

"Well, where I come from women don't spend the night with two strange men."

He smirked. "Guess they don't know what they're missing."

She bit her bottom lip and refused to look him in the eye. Parker prided himself on being a good judge of character. He expected her type to be overly confident with a huge ego. If he didn't know better, he'd say she was on the shy side with a healthy dose of insecurity.

"Don't mind him, Robyn. Come on in." Yukon got her inside far enough that he could shut the side door. The resulting silence was awkward and deafening.

"I'm sorry to put you out. It's unlike my friend to ditch me like that … in the middle of nowhere. Then again, this was our first assignment away from home."

Parker set his bottle down and proceeded to walk around the room. He didn't take his eyes off their houseguest. Her sweet feminine scent had already infused itself in the air, their masculine domain invaded by her presence. Parker practically salivated thinking of all the things he'd like to do with her—to her.

"Why would your friend leave you in our town?" asked Yukon, offering her a spot on the sofa. She tentatively sat down, crossing those long, smooth legs. He'd always been a sucker for high heels, and hers had to be a good five inches long.

"I'm sure she had a good reason, but that doesn't help my case much. We were supposed to get some papers signed and look into local boundary disputes, but we were late and our contact was already gone."

"And she just left you at the diner?"

Robyn shrugged. "She said she'd be right back. If I had of known this would happen, I would have made sure to get my purse from her car ... or not come out here at all."

"I'm glad you came," said Yukon, his voice taking on a deeper tone. The love-struck look in his brother's eyes reminded Parker that Robyn had to be off the appetizer menu. If he tried to get her into his bed, Yukon would never forgive him. They'd fought tooth and nail over women before, but that was when they were both young and stupid. Yet as hard as he tried, his feet wouldn't carry him away and his eyes wouldn't divert from the busty brunette.

He decided to lighten the mood with regular conversation and keep things civil. She was in a strange place, out of her element. "You're probably talking about the oil pipeline. A lot of farmers are against it because it'll cross their land."

"I assure you that many are for it," she said like a programmed lawyer. The topic wasn't personal to him because the pipeline didn't pass through their fields, but he could empathize with his distant neighbors. These city folk only cared about money, even more than legacy, land kept in a family for countless generations. Their own house might be a shithole, but it was home and he'd tell any legal team to fuck off if they demanded he sell.

"From what I hear, farmers aren't going along willingly. It's not as simple as dollars and cents—" He wanted to tell her to get off her high horse and actually talk with people affected rather than reading some legal reports.

"Parker," Yukon warned, as if reading his mind.

His brother was right, of course. He needed to keep his mouth shut. Ms. Fancy Pants might be a high-priced lawyer, but she was also a woman, vulnerable and alone. It was late, and he was overworked and overtired. Add sex-starved to the list and he was one ornery cowboy.

"I'll be upstairs if you need me." He slipped away, heading upstairs to his bedroom. Yukon could play with his city toy in peace. Parker hoped he was smart enough to realize she'd never look back once she got a ride out of their dusty little town.

****

Robyn bit the inside of her cheek nearly to the point of bleeding, a nervous habit she needed to break. She wanted to be anywhere else, well almost anywhere. At least she was inside, warm, and safe from the elements and wildlife. Other than that, her situation was nightmarish. She felt like a criminal—tried and convicted, based on nothing more than her position. These guys didn't realize that she was powerless on every count. She was a pencil pusher, a dime-a-dozen paralegal in a huge firm. Nobody even remembered her name. Her convictions or ideals counted for nothing. She did what she was told or she would be out a job, and success meant everything to her.

Calloway said the farmers were happy to get cash for their rundown farms. She could have argued with Parker, but she wasn't dumb enough to get into a heated debate when she didn't have all the facts.

Robyn watched as Parker left the room. His towel sat low on his hips, showcasing a strong, lean physique. God, why did he have to have such a hard body? It would be so much easier to ignore him. She'd tried to focus anywhere than his chest and ripped abs, but still managed to memorize many details, including the numerous old scars. He moved with the stealth of wild cat, every shifting muscle fascinating her. She wanted to hate him, just like she wanted to hate Yukon—but failed. While she might be a trembling mess on the outside, her hormones were definitely working on overdrive. Robyn couldn't be blamed for her rising temperature. Any sighted woman would be helpless to resist.

Only one problem—she convinced herself the only male she'd ever be attracted to would be one in a designer suit. It was what she wanted and demanded. She was angry with her body and those impossible-to-ignore desires. The sight of these two rough and tumble cowboys—scars, calloused hands, and all—make her feel truly feminine. They made her want to take a bite of the forbidden fruit, the same one she swore she'd never partake in. The place even smelled like the essence of a man, something woodsy and all masculine. *Shelly would laugh her ass off if she saw me drooling over cowboys.* She recalled her recent conversation with Shelly, the one about a happily ever after. Was her friend right? Was love an illusion?

Chapter Six

Yukon showed her a spare room where she could sleep. At least they weren't forcing themselves on her. In a small way, she was disappointed. Maybe a big way. If she couldn't get a backwoods hillbilly to put the moves on her, she must have some serious desirability issues. She imagined she looked like shit after the hellish day she'd endured. As much as she wanted to check a mirror, she had no hair brush or make-up for damage control regardless.

"It's not too big, but the bed's comfortable," Yukon said, holding the door open wide for her.

She entered the room. A lightbulb dangled from the ceiling, making the room appear to be moving on waves. It wasn't what she was used to. Her circle of friends and co-workers demanded the best of everything. They'd never be caught dead in a room with water stains, peeling wallpaper, and questionable bedding.

"Thank you," she said, walking to the head of the bed. Robyn fluffed the pillow and suddenly noticed her reflection from the dark curtain-less window. She looked like a fish out of water with her full business suit. It made her wonder what everyone else in this town thought of her.

He must have noticed her hesitation. "It's probably not what you're used to."

"Not exactly." Did that sound rude? She turned to look at him. He was a presence, most of the doorway filled with his strong body. His face had a sun-kissed glow, and even with the minimal lighting in the room, his blue eyes were piercing.

"Sorry about that, darlin'. We aren't used to having a woman under the roof. Not that I'm complaining." He licked his lower lip, and her pussy clenched.

"Hopefully I'll be out of your hair first thing in the morning." She just finished speaking when a loud rap at the window made her yelp.

"What in God's name?" Yukon took a few brisk strides to the window and hoisted up the heavy wooden frame. It was pouring out, a mix of heavy rain and hail. The entire evening she'd been sitting outside the diner, it had been dry and dusty, not a cloud in the starry night sky. Now this?

Someone bounded up the stairs, the hollow echo reaching them in the little room. A breathless Parker rushed in, joining his brother at the window.

"I heard about this on the radio. It must be the storm tearing through the south end. I sure as hell didn't expect it to pay us a visit."

Yukon pulled the window back down and secured the lock. "Will the roof hold?"

Parker shrugged.

She could feel the tension and worry in the air like a living force. Robyn just stood there, an outsider looking in, and wondered if Shelly and Peter were okay.

"Shit, I haven't finished clearing the east fields," Yukon said.

"Nothing we can do about that now. I'm sure we're not the only ones caught off guard."

They both turned to her at once as if they'd both forgotten she was still in the room. She'd only seen these men as empty-headed flirts and didn't expect anything monumental during her one-night stay. Now a new side to them unfolded in front of her—an intensity that took her breath away.

"Don't worry, Robyn. We'll take good care of you," said Yukon. Parker said nothing, but continued staring at her.

"What's wrong? It's just rain, isn't it?"

Parker ran a hand through his hair, moving toward her. "If it's the storm closing roads south of us, we'll wish it was just rain." When he was right in front of her, she had to crane her neck to look up. Had she even seen a man with shoulders that broad? "Don't tell me a tough-as-nails city girl is afraid of a country storm."

Did he notice the tremble in her voice? Was she so transparent that he could see through her false bravado?

She shook her head. How could these simple cowboys have so much control over her? She'd always equated power and dominance with money and status, not the look in a man's eyes. Parker had her speechless, his presence larger than life. The thin flannel of his shirt hugged those muscular shoulders. She guessed he'd earned every muscle from hard work rather than visits to a gym during lunch hour. It didn't help that she'd already seen him in the bare flesh.

A screeching whine saved her from his spell. They all looked up as the lights snapped off with a resounding zap. She screamed and ducked her head as shards of glass rained down on them. Deafening silence blanketed the room once the drone of electricity was put to rest. Without thinking, she reached out and grabbed Parker's arm in a death grip.

"Well, fuck me." Parker growled his displeasure. "Get the flashlights and candles. I'll secure the horses and windows."

She heard Yukon leave the room, moving as if he had night vision, but she guessed he'd lived in this old house his whole life. It was something she'd never known herself, but could imagine. Parker turned her around and pushed her down to sit on the edge of the bed. "You wait here until we get sorted, okay? I'll bring up a lantern."

"Okay."

She didn't want to be left alone in the dark bedroom, but had no choice but to put her trust in these two strangers. Her lonely apartment in the city actually seemed appealing at this point. At least she had safety, electricity, and no unacceptable temptations tearing down her ideals. Without light, all her senses were magnified. Rain pelted the thin glass and tin roof. The rest of the world, including the one she'd left behind, all started to seem like a distant memory. She was once again a vulnerable young girl, her fate not yet mapped out for her. If only life was that simple.

She could hear the faint sound of voices from the brothers downstairs. They were moving around with urgency, window shutters slapping shut from outside, and cupboards being searched. Were Shelly and Peter stranded in the storm, trapped by a road block? Her mind tried to make excuses to ease the anger she held for them.

After a while, Robyn's eyes adjusted to the darkness and she attempted to walk to the window. There was nothing but blackness beyond, no hint of a moon, stars, or life. She placed her hand on the glass—the cool, moist surface forcing her back to the past. A great sadness seeped from that locked place in her heart. She abruptly pulled away, walking backward until the backs of her knees hit the bed. She sat down on the mattress. *I have to get out of here.* Robyn couldn't spend the night in another strange house in another strange bed. She was tired of new smells, new sounds, and trying to decipher new personalities. She never should have agreed to come to this little town.

"Are you okay?"

She whirled around, still sitting on the edge of the

bed. Yukon was only feet away, holding some sort of old oil lamp in an outstretched hand. The concerned look on his face made her realize her heart was racing and breathing rapid. She mentally tried to calm herself, to remember she was an adult in control of her own destiny.

"Yeah, I just... Yeah, I'm okay."

He set the lantern on the wooden dresser and came to sit next to her on the bed. His weight made the springs whine and mattress dip. She started to slide into him, but righted her position.

"We've secured the house, the cellar is stocked full, and we have enough firewood to last four seasons if it decides to get cold. Nothing to worry about." His voice was calm and reassuring. She started to feel guilty for judging these men on their social class without even knowing a thing about them. Her prejudice was deeply ingrained.

"I'm not worried."

"But you're crying." Yukon reached out and ran the backs of his fingers along her cheek. She could see the moisture glisten on his skin in the lamp light. Had she actually been crying? She hated that a simple memory could strip her down to the marrow.

"I'm not," she lied.

He narrowed his eyes. "Tell me what's wrong. I'll try my best to fix it."

She chuckled without humor, and replied without thinking. "This, you can't fix." Then she thought better. "Forget I said that."

There was silence for a couple minutes. The wavering lantern light made eerie shadows along the wall in front of them, demons of the past ready to devour her whole.

"My brother thinks you're a spoiled little rich girl used to getting what you want. A lawyer with a bank account large enough to buy our town and then some. Is he right?"

"Sure, Yukon, whatever you say."

He exhaled as if exasperated. "Tell me something, Robyn. I know there's more to you than meets the eye."

What did she have to lose? She'd never see these men again after tomorrow. "Well for starters, I'm not a lawyer. I'm a paralegal."

"Those are different?"

She smiled. "Yes, very different. Well, when it comes to the bank account part."

"And the spoiled part?"

Robyn shook her head. "Couldn't be further from the truth. I'm not even sure how that would feel."

"I don't understand," he said. She could hear the genuine concern in his voice, which was surprising since he barely knew her. Unfortunately for him, she wasn't ready to share her dysfunctional life story.

"Never mind. I'm just tired. Way too tired." She stood up and returned to the window to get away from Yukon and his questions. What was it about the night that brought out all her vulnerabilities? It was an endless cycle of highs and lows when all she wanted was stability.

"I promise I won't bite," he said. "You can tell me anything."

She could feel his presence right behind her, so close. Her mental state was too fragile for kindness. City life suited her because nobody gave a shit about anyone else. Keeping her mental health under tight control, only her perfected exterior available for view, was her survival mechanism.

He touched her hair, and she instinctively flinched away.

"I told you she was skittish," said Parker. She turned to see him entering the room with a broom and dustpan. Why was his shirt off again? *Holy shit, he's so ripped.* Her mind became blank as she stared at the golden cowboy, his damp hair casually slicked back and his skin gleaming from the rain. "Don't waste your time, Yukon. She thinks she's too good for you. Maybe she is."

Robyn frowned, her cheeks heating as she roughly tugged off her suit jacket. She balled it up and threw it down on the bed. "There, is that better? Stop judging me by my appearance. You don't know anything about me."

Rather than appear shocked or sobered after her embarrassing little outburst, it appeared to have amused him. The fact only made her angrier. Back in the city, it took a painful amount of effort just to squeak by when she was surrounded by human Barbie dolls. Here in the backwoods, she was judged as superior just for wearing a half-priced suit. It should have pleased her but rather it insulted her to the core. No matter where she was, she never fit in.

"Don't stop there. Take it all off, baby girl."

Robyn growled. "You're impossible!"

How could a man be desirable and repellent at the same time? She wanted to fight and argue, but deep down she knew Parker wasn't to blame. It surprised her how easily these men could break down the walls around her emotions. Or was it this place? She was a fucking mess.

"Leave her be," said Yukon. "She's been crying."

Parker narrowed his eyes and moved close enough that he could tilt her chin up. She tried to move her head to the side but he wouldn't have it. "You know I'm playing, don't you?"

He actually sounded sincere, his playful quality no longer present. The scent of fresh rain and his musky cologne were an inviting aphrodisiac.

She exhaled heavily, suddenly realizing how fast her heart was racing. It was difficult for her to accept kindness, even though she craved it. "I'm sorry. I'm overtired and stressed out. This isn't me."

Parker smiled, tucking loose hairs behind her ear. "Nothing to be sorry about. I'm the one who needs to mind his manners. Come on…" He led her to the bed and pulled back the heavy patchwork quilt. "A good night's sleep will do us all a world of good."

They started to head to the door after Parker swept up the broken glass from the lightbulb. Yukon turned back briefly before leaving. "If you need anything, just shout. I'm in the next room over."

Once alone, she flopped down on the bed and rubbed her hands over her face. Sleep would bring back her composure and a new day would give her the strength she desperately needed.

She hoped.

Chapter Seven

After a fitful night's sleep, Yukon reached the bottom of the stairs and found Parker in the kitchen. The power was still out. His brother dumped a stock pot full of water into the kitchen sink.

"What's going on?"

"Go see for yourself," he said after another curse. "Basement's flooded and the rain's not letting up."

He looked to the window. Even though it was eight in the morning, it looked more like dusk. The thick cloud cover blocked out the sun, and rain fell in torrents. Strong winds shook the house, howling as it breached the cracks in the old structure. He couldn't believe their little town was a dust bowl only a day earlier.

"What's the plan?" Yukon asked.

Parker snorted as he left the kitchen with the empty pot. "Get bailing!"

Shit. Their roof was a patch job he doubted would hold up for long and their basement wasn't properly weatherproofed. Even during small rain storms, they'd get flooded. This weather system would put their old house to the test. He began to catalog all the tasks they'd put off over the past year, now wishing he hadn't procrastinated.

Yukon grabbed a glass of orange juice before joining his brother. It would have been pitch black in the basement if not for the lantern precariously hanging from the ceiling. Water reached past his ankles, plastic containers floating by. He squeezed by his brother and reached for an empty bucket. The sound of sloshing water reminded him of summers by the lake when he was a kid. Now it was just him, Parker, and memories. And a flooded basement.

It was punishing work hauling the heavy loads up and down the flight of rickety wooden stairs. Each time he tossed a bucket out the front door, the rain soaked the foyer. He was so lost in his task, passing Parker on the stairs time and time again, that he'd forgotten about their houseguest.

"What's happening?" Robyn asked after he shut the front door for what felt like the thousandth time.

He set his bucket down for a minute and decided it was a good time to take a breather.

"Sump pump isn't working because of the power outage, and we can't fire up the gas generator until we get some of the water bailed out."

"A flood? The power's still out? Is that normal?"

He chuckled, the panic in her voice endearing. "Darlin', nothing about the past day is normal, but we'll get by. Not a thing to worry about."

She frowned, running one hand over the other arm as if to comfort herself. "But I was supposed to leave this morning. I have to get to work. I need a working phone. I—"

Parker reached the main floor with another bucket. Yukon opened the door for him, closing it a few seconds later. "Good morning to you, little miss. Although there ain't too much good about it, is there?"

"How long is this storm going to last? I have to get back to the city."

"You're free to leave." Parker waved his arm to the entrance.

Robyn scowled, but a sudden burst of explosive thunder made her gasp and brace a hand against the wall.

Yukon felt the need to comfort her, to make everything right in her world. He wasn't sure what it was about Robyn, but the attraction he felt for her was strong and undeniable. "It's not safe to be out in that storm.

With the power out, there could easily be more road closures."

"I can't believe this is happening."

Was it that bad to be stuck in his house? What would it take to please an educated woman like Robyn? Did he even possess what she needed?

"Sorry to disappoint," said Parker. "But this is real life in the country. You work with what you're dealt or you die complaining."

Their bailing wasn't getting them anywhere. The storm was abusing the old house. They needed to do something different if they wanted to make it through another day or longer. "How about we use the plastic from the hay baler and wrap the basement?"

Parker stopped in his tracks, not saying a word. Before he even spoke, Yukon knew he liked the idea. They were too much in sync, living together day in day out their entire lives.

"That won't be an easy task—if it even works. It's crazy, actually."

"What do we have to lose? Even if it takes the edge off, it'll be a help so we can get the generator and sump pump going."

Parker nodded and reached for his overcoat hanging beside the door. "Hang tight, baby girl." He winked at their houseguest before heading into the fury of the rain storm.

"Should I do something?" Robyn asked, looking bewildered.

He felt guilty because, despite her desperation to leave, he was glad they were holed up together. As he tugged on his flannel jacket, he nodded to the staircase. "While we have a bit of light, can you check the closets upstairs? I know we have some extra lanterns and oil around here somewhere. I'm sure we'll need them tonight."

****

Tonight? That meant these cowboys had no hope in getting her home any time soon, certainly not today. She wasn't sure how she should feel. Part of her felt like having a toddler-style meltdown. Another part revelled in the escape from reality. It didn't hurt that Yukon and Parker were two of the hardest, sexiest men she'd ever seen in the flesh. If she were honest with herself, she'd admit the two brothers made her feel things Peter and other refined men at the office never could. She'd always promised herself never to fall for a working-class stiff. But it was wishful thinking if she believed the sight of these cowboys was a turn-off. In fact, just the way they looked at her made her uncomfortably achy. How long had it been since a man could do that to her?

Robyn felt odd being alone in the big old home. The rain beat against the house, the echo from the tin roof creating a static sound that was almost soothing. She made her way up the old staircase, holding the handrail because it was difficult to see in the darkened corridor. Where should she start? She'd been given free rein to snoop, so she was going to take advantage of it.

She started in Yukon's bedroom since it was next to the room she'd slept in. Well, she'd tried to sleep. Most of the night Robyn had tossed and turned, old memories and insecurities driving her crazy. It had been years since she'd slept in a strange bed and it shocked her how much it still affected her. She felt like a vulnerable child, not a grown woman traveling on business.

As soon as she pushed open the door, the first thing she noticed was the faint and delicious scent of his cologne. She took a deep breath as she entered, Yukon's essence invading her senses. She wanted to drown in it. The curtains were drawn, so she tugged them open to let in the meager amount of light. Everything was simplistic, the furniture all made from solid wood. There wasn't a modern piece to be found. She slowly walked around, taking everything in. There were some pictures on a tall wardrobe. She stretched up on her tiptoes to get a look. They were family photos with Yukon and Parker as boys. They were handsome even as children—little cowboys. She wondered what their story was and if their parents were still living.

Why hadn't they married? Or had they? She had so many questions that really weren't any of her business.

Before moving on, she ran a finger along the thick dust. The place could use a thorough cleaning, or more like a complete home makeover. She opened the closet and did a quick scan for the lanterns, even though she couldn't care less about her task. The clothes hanging were different versions of the same long-sleeved plaid shirt and a few t-shirts. There was a large cardboard box on the floor so she crouched down and peeked inside.

Robyn wanted to find something significant that would give her a snapshot into these men's lives. She shouldn't care, but still needed to learn more. The box was full of sweaters, a big disappointment. Robyn sighed, wondering where to look next. Parker's room felt like it was off limits, even though nothing had been said one way or the other. If his bedroom had a closet, then she was obligated to investigate, or so she told herself.

She listened to ensure they hadn't come back inside yet, then she opened the door to Parker's room across the hall. It felt like entering forbidden territory. Her senses were heightened and her heart began to pound. Being in Parker's private domain did strange things to her libido. When she saw his queen-sized bed with rumpled navy sheets, her pussy tingled. How many women had warmed his bed? She wondered if cowboys even settled down. Businessmen sure seemed to be playboys for life. And why the hell did she care one way or the other?

Robyn tiptoed around the room, looking for anything off limits. She didn't know what she expected to find, but when she saw a shoe box in the top shelf of his closet, she immediately reached for it. It was heavy, so she knew it contained more than an extra pair of shoes. She sat on the edge of his bed and carefully opened the lid. There was an assortment of old fringed photos and small trinkets inside. It was difficult to see with the minimal light. She picked up a silver belt buckle, holding it in the direction of the window to get a better look. Many of the pictures featured a beautiful, dark-haired woman. Her heart sank a bit, knowing his heart probably belonged to her, but she was being ridiculous, of course. Maybe she really did have fairy tale sickness.

She continued to rummage through the contents. There was a small jewelry box. Inside was an intricately designed ring, either silver or white gold encrusted with tiny diamonds. She studied it absently, wondering who it belonged to or who it was intended for. A bang from downstairs gave her system a jolt. Robyn panicked as she tried to get everything back into the box in record time. She jumped to her feet and reached up to get the forbidden treasure back on the top shelf.

"Looking for something?"

Fuck! The voice was impossibly deep, the essence of a man. She wasn't sure if she should be terrified or turned on.

She whirled around after barely getting the shoebox back into place. Parker was leaning against the doorframe, his arms crossed over his chest. He didn't look angry, but not amused either. How had he gotten upstairs so fast?

"I–I was looking for a lantern. Yukon told me to check every room…" She was still breathless and not concealing the fact very well.

He still hadn't moved. "Did you have any luck?"

She shook her head slowly, feeling like a naughty child caught in the act. He was dripping wet, his hair pushed casually off his face. He was striking, a man with intensity and presence. When she didn't speak, he proceeded to unfold his arms and enter the dim room.

Parker slowly tugged the soaking shirt up over his head, tossing it in a hamper near his bed. His muscles looked strained and defined, glistening from the moisture. She couldn't stop staring, wishing she could lick those drips of water off his skin. When he turned away, she noticed his back was wide and lean-muscled, marred with scars and fresh bruises. He sat down heavily on the end of the bed and pulled off his socks, going about his business as if she weren't even there. When he stood to unbuckle his belt, she let out an involuntary squeak.

He froze, directing a glance at her. "Problem?"

"What are you doing?"

"I've been working my ass off in that devil of a storm for nearly an hour. I'm cold, I'm wet, and if you haven't noticed, this is my bedroom."

"Oh." She felt like an idiot. He wasn't going to hit on her. She was just in the wrong place at the wrong time. She should be thankful he hadn't called her out for snooping. "I'll leave you alone then."

She bolted in the direction of the door, but Parker moved faster, bracing one arm across the only exit. "I didn't tell you to leave." Robyn now noticed the tattooed letters along his inner arm. God, he was drool-worthy.

"But—"

They were so close. She'd almost crashed into his chest in her escape attempt. She could even smell him, an all-male scent that made her salivate. "What do you think of me, baby girl?"

She narrowed her eyes. "I don't know what you mean."

"How do I compare to men in the city?"

Did he actually just ask that? "In what way?"

He smirked, a slight dimple appearing on his cheek. "Not too bright, are you?"

She scowled. "I'm not going to stroke your ego. The county girls might drool over your muscles or think you're God's gift to women, but I know better."

Parker ran his tongue over his teeth, staring down at her with a mix of amusement and intensity. "I was talking about my hospitality, but I like where you're taking things, sugar. God's gift, eh?"

Her face heated so hot, her cheeks had to be flushed crimson. She wanted to bite her tongue … right off.

"No smart comebacks? I'm surprised." He lowered his arm from the doorway and began to stalk forward, effectively forcing her to walk awkwardly backward. "But, then again, everything about you surprises me."

When her back hit the closet door, she gasped. His perfect bare chest was so close, his abs ripped even at rest. Every time he moved, his unfastened belt buckle jangled, and the band of his boxers was visible. Her control was shot because all she wanted to do was reach out and touch him. The urge became more and more undeniable. She thought about Trey from accounting, a temptation she was smart enough to avoid. Parker would require a new level of self-restraint, and she wasn't even sure any woman possessed that much power.

"I–I didn't mean what I said. I mean, it's not what you think…"

She looked up to gauge his reaction. He had a gentle smile on his lips, one so irresistible she hoped he'd steal a kiss. Or a hell of a lot more.

"You have no idea the things I'd like to do to you." He ran his hand through her hair, a little too rough. This guy was completely no holds barred, and she loved that the political correctness she was used to from men was nowhere to be found. He lowered his head close enough that she could hear him breathing. "You're everything I should avoid, but I can't seem to keep you off my mind."

You and me both, she thought. She wanted to scream for him to take what he wanted. She'd worry about the repercussions tomorrow. Right now she needed this cowboy all over her. She wanted them naked and so entangled that it would be indistinguishable where one started and the other began. Robyn would never see these country boys again, so why not indulge in the fantasy of a lifetime?

"Some days I wish I wasn't such a good brother." He stepped back, holding his arm open to allow her to exit his room.

What the hell? "What are you saying?"

"I know you're smarter than that. Anyone can see my brother's crazy about you."

She was at a complete loss, trying to piece everything together while tamping down her wild libido. She was wound up tight, ready to jump into bed with Parker, no questions asked—so unlike her. Now Robyn was forced to think about things besides sex, like the other hot guy who lived in the same house. "You're wrong. I don't even know him. He tried to hit on me, that's it."

Parker chuckled. "I know Yukon. He's a love-sick puppy. So have a heart and keep your distance. We both know you have no interest in men like us."

Her mouth parted but no words came out. He was actually worried she'd break his brother's heart? She was the victim in all this—trapped and helpless in a strange little town. God, he made her feel like some perverted, heartless freak from the city. The fact she'd only thought about muscles and broad shoulders since arriving made her feel worse. How could Yukon have feelings from her beyond lust? They were strangers. Love at first sight was a theme from fairy tales, not reality. Or were country boys so hard up for women, they'd grab onto the first one to walk into their dusty town?

Chapter Eight

It should have been simple—a quick fuck with a beautiful, willing woman. Only it wasn't simple at all. He told himself he was taking the higher road, keeping his hands to himself for the sake of Yukon. But since when had he ever passed up an easy piece of pussy?

This woman had gotten into his head. It was easy to believe he'd avoided her for his brother's sake, but it was more than that. Somehow he knew Robyn would be his undoing. She brought out his deep-seated insecurities. City women had always treated him like shit when he traveled the circuit, assuming cowboys were brainless and only good for one thing. One in particular had stomped on his heart, making him cautious to this day. People from the city weren't superior, they were assholes.

Robyn was different. She might have a fancy suit and high-priced education, but he could see beneath the layers. This girl was damaged, insecure, and for some reason she wanted *him*. He could practically taste her, her desire affecting him like some kind of drug. As much as he wanted her in his bed, she was too complicated. She was from a different world, and he knew getting involved with her would be a mistake. It was better to keep his distance until the damn rain let up so Robyn could get back to her real life.

Parker was freshening up in the bathroom when the lights snapped on. With the generator kicking in, they could dry out the basement and have the basic necessities. And he'd have to face Robyn again. A war waged in his mind—to give in or stay strong. He'd been mother and father to Yukon for too many years to count. Although he was only two years older than his brother, he'd taken on personal responsibility for Yukon. The least Parker could do was save his little brother the heartache he knew Robyn would give him.

Their houseguest wasn't comfortable in her less-than-stellar accommodations, so there was no way she'd be interested in an uneducated cowboy. She'd been stressing about getting back to the city, so there was no point for Yukon to get his hopes up. Any connection they made would be severed as soon as she could get a ride back to her reality.

He'd just dried his face when Yukon burst into the small bathroom, nearly barreling him down. "Generator's working!"

Parker pushed past him. "I kind of figured that one out. With the lights and all."

"Well, I sure as hell didn't expect it to start up so soon. Things are definitely looking up." Yukon had a goofy smile on his face. He was no doubt dreaming of Robyn again.

Parker leaned against the door frame, listening to ensure they were alone upstairs. "Listen, Yukon. When she leaves, she won't look back. A girl like Robyn isn't meant for country living." Parker didn't want to hurt Yukon, but his fantasy needed a dose of reality.

"You don't know anything about her," he snapped.

"I know her type. She'll probably fuck anything that walks. That doesn't make you special."

"Why do you always think the worst of everyone? Or is it you just can't stand to see me happy?"

He did want Yukon happy, but unlike him, Parker wasn't so easy to trust. His brother had never ventured out of their closed community, while he'd traveled the circuit and seen the darker side of humanity. Not all women were sugar and spice.

"I'm just giving you facts. Listen, don't listen ... whatever. Just don't come bitching to me when you find out I'm right," said Parker.

"She's different. I can feel it."

"It still doesn't mean she's ready to trade her briefcase for an egg basket. Use your head before you make a mistake you'll regret."

"I'm not a fucking kid, Parker. You don't need to look out for me. I've been with plenty of women, and I've yet to shed a tear."

That was true. Yukon had taken his fair share of women, local and passing through, to bed. He never wanted anything more than sex, never looked at any of them the way he looked at Robyn. What did it mean? Was it a mid-life crisis?

Regardless, Robyn had been ready and willing to give Parker a home run, so she couldn't have special feelings for Yukon. He wished things were different, wished Yukon could find the happiness he deserved. But Robyn wasn't the answer.

Robyn started to walk up the stairs, the creak in the fifth step an alarm they both knew well. They'd been trouble to the tenth degree growing up, putting their father through hell and back. When their dad would come upstairs to give them the belt, that same creak turned their blood to ice. Now it was all bitter-sweet memories.

They both stood still, not saying a word.

"The power's back," said Robyn as she reached the top of the landing. "That's a good sign."

"Hear that hum? It's just the generator kicking on. The power's not back to the town yet," said Parker.

It pissed him off that Robyn was so anxious to get home when he knew Yukon was ready to sell his soul to make her happy.

"What can we do?" she asked.

Parker smirked. There wasn't much space at the top of the stairs, all three of them only feet apart. "What do you *want* to do?"

She looked at him, unblinking, no doubt remembering their time alone. "If we can't leave, I guess we wait it out."

Yukon stepped between them. "You hungry, darlin'?"

Robyn nodded.

So, the little princess ate like the rest of them. He doubted she'd be impressed with anything they could offer her. She probably lived off sushi and weird fancy shit, not beef stew and potatoes.

They made their way downstairs, and Parker was surprised when Yukon led her to the formal dining room. Since their mother died, they'd never used that room. It was frozen in time ever since their father refused to use it, and it became the norm in their home.

Yukon snapped off the protective sheet from the large wooden table. "Have a seat, Robyn. Don't worry about a thing." His brother winked at their guest and shoulder bumped him as he left the dining room.

Parker gripped the back of Robyn's chair with both hands, leaning down to whisper in her ear from behind. "Don't lead him on. Hopefully we'll have you back on your way soon."

****

Robyn whirled around in her seat. "Excuse me?"

"Yukon won't listen to my warnings, so I'm telling you."

She glared at him. Back home, she was invisible compared to the women she worked with. For Parker to think she was some man-eater was laughable. Besides, despite her best efforts, there was something about

Yukon that called out to her. If things were different, maybe another lifetime, she could see herself falling for a rugged cowboy like him. But like Shelly had told her, this was reality, and Prince Charming didn't exist.

Robyn knew exactly what she needed, and it wasn't either of these two men. They'd destroy everything she'd worked so hard for. Make her relive a dysfunctional cycle she was trying to break free of.

"I'm not interested in either of you. If it wasn't for this storm, I'd be long gone."

"My point exactly."

She turned back around in her chair, heat creeping up her collar. *What an asshole!*

Parker took a seat across from her as Yukon came back into the room.

"Stew is warming up. Shouldn't be long," he said, sitting and folding his hands on the table. He stared at her, the intensity making her feel like she was being stripped, layer by layer. If it wasn't for the rain breaking the silent hush, she would have been able to hear them all breathing. She knew Parker was watching her, too, judging her every move.

"So … how long have you been farming?" she asked Yukon. Small talk was better than uncomfortable silence.

"All our lives. The farm was passed down to us. It's the only thing we know."

She bit her lower lip, thinking of more safe topics. "Do you like it? Farming, I mean."

Yukon smiled. "There ain't much choice in the matter, besides, I'd never abandon the family farm … or our town."

"Have you ever been anywhere else?" she asked.

"No need."

"The city's not what it's cracked up to be, either.

The grass isn't always greener," said Parker, chiming in.

"It's not so bad. I like the chaos," Robyn said.

"I'd go crazy living out here. It's too isolated, too quiet."

"What you hiding from?" asked Yukon.

Robyn felt like he could see everything, even her darkest secrets. As far as they knew, she was a perfectly normal woman in their town on business. "Why would you ask that?"

"Our father always told us that a man afraid of silence is hiding from his demons."

She swallowed hard. Robyn didn't have demons, not really. Her childhood had been fucked up, and she missed the mark as an adult, but that wasn't the same.

Or was it?

She liked the chaos because … she didn't want to remember anything. And it helped her forget the loneliness.

"I don't have demons. I just like a certain lifestyle," she said, trying to convince herself as much as them.

Even the rain couldn't kill the white noise this time. She squirmed in her seat as both men assessed her. Why did she feel like this was an interrogation?

"What kind of lifestyle is that?" asked Parker. "Everything money can buy?"

"Maybe," she snapped.

"Then I guarantee you, that's not much at all." Parker smirked at her. "A little time away from the big smoke might be just what the doctor ordered. Around these parts, our motto is hard work and loyalty."

"There's nothing wrong with me," she whispered.

Yukon cleared his throat. "I'll get the food. That's a good start to feeling like yourself." He glared at his brother. Now that he'd mentioned food, she realized how hungry she was. The rich, savory scent hung heavily in the air.

Alone with Parker again.

They had a stare off, and she hated how vulnerable he made her feel. And despite the rift between them, he still made her horny. He ran a hand through his damp hair, looking too sexy for an asshole. "Why do you hate me so much? You don't even know me," she said.

He didn't answer her, but undressed her with his eyes, a slow, sensual assault.

She whispered harshly so Yukon couldn't hear them. "And I'm not some kind of whore like you make me out to be. I'm sure you're both way more experienced than me."

"Is that so? Just how many men have you had, Robyn?"

"That's none of your business." She crossed her arms, her jaw clenched down tight.

He tilted his head to the side. "And still not married?"

"Neither are you."

"Touché." He wet his lips, leaning over on his forearms. Very hard, muscular forearms. "Why is a beautiful woman from the city still single?"

The way he said *beautiful* left no room for argument. He meant it, a matter of fact, not just a word. For some reason, a compliment from Parker felt priceless.

"Because where I work and play, the women are perfect. Men expect it, and women change themselves to meet those expectations."

"Not you?"

"Not yet."

He frowned, his teasing quality fading. "What do you mean by changing? I can't see a thing wrong with you, darlin'."

"Well, I don't know about the women in your town, but where I'm from they consider me overweight." She felt her cheeks heat with embarrassment. "And old."

"Then the men in the city are fools. They obviously don't know how to handle a real woman." Once again, the mood they'd created in his bedroom was back. Robyn felt entranced by the cowboy, ready to submit body and soul—so unlike her.

She was going to fish for more compliments when Yukon entered the room with two bowls. He set one down in front of her and sat down with the other.

Parker grumbled and left the room.

"It's all homemade. It was our mother's recipe," said Yukon.

"Smells great," she said, giving the stew a stir. At this point, she'd eat anything. "Do you mind me asking about your parents?"

The brothers weren't old. She guessed in their forties.

After his first bite of stew, he answered. "Our mother died when we were just boys. She would have been around our age when she passed. Her death broke something in our father. He never remarried, never moved on. We still say he died of a broken heart."

"Wow, I'm so sorry. That's the saddest thing I've ever heard."

He smirked, but it didn't reach his eyes. "I keep promising myself I won't end up like him, you know, dying alone. But here I am, heading down the same road."

"Don't say that," she said. "Any woman would be happy to have you."

He stared at her, making her breath catch.

"What if I want you?" he asked.

The moment was emotionally charged. She

thought of her own life and battle with loneliness. She didn't want to hurt him, especially after everything Parker had told her, but she knew she couldn't go down this path. Her mind had become clouded, reality fading away the longer she stayed with the brothers. But once she got back to the city, this would all be a memory.

"I hardly know you, Yukon. I'm talking about women here, in your own town."

"I'm not interested in any of them," he said, before continuing to eat his food. She did the same, and she wondered if the topic was closed.

Robyn watched Yukon eat, sneaking discreet peeks. He had a strong jaw, rough with stubble—such masculine features. His upper body was built like a brick house, his shirt clinging to all those home-grown muscles. Why wasn't she falling head-over-heels for this cowboy's attention? She knew everything about him was sincere, unlike the bastards back home who only wanted in her pants. It was her own ideals and expectations that kept putting on the brakes. She couldn't give up now, not after a lifetime of struggling to make something of herself.

Chapter Nine

"Feel better?" Yukon asked.

Robyn came down the stairs, still towel drying her hair. She looked adorable wearing his John Deere t-shirt and rolled up sweatpants.

She smiled. "A shower can certainly do wonders." Robyn walked to the big picture window. "What's the forecast today?"

The storm hadn't hit them as bad as the south, and it already appeared to be petering out. He'd already been out first thing in the morning to check on the state of their fields. It looked like they were one of the lucky farms.

"Rain. Then some more rain," he said.

"Great." She didn't sound disappointed like she'd been yesterday. Almost playful. Comfortable. "What are your plans for today?"

"I can't waste away another day. I've got to get some work done outside, rain or shine, and I need to check on a neighbor."

She nodded. "I can help. Well, I can try."

He liked the idea of toting Robyn around. Being seen with her would only make him proud. Yukon had a laundry list of chores he had to tackle, and hated the idea of leaving Robyn alone most of the day. He hadn't made much headway in winning her over. She still seemed repelled by country living.

The front door opened, the sound of rain briefly filling the room, until it was shut out with a bang. Parker hung up his overcoat and used a hand to ruffle his hair. "Nasty out there."

Robyn just stared at him.

"You should have something to eat before we

head out," Yukon told Robyn. "There's oatmeal on the stove."

"Where you two going?" asked Parker. He kicked off his boots and entered the kitchen, pouring himself a mug of coffee.

"I need to check on Ms. Granger, then I have to mend one of the fences behind the barn. A downed tree busted it open."

"We can cut it up for firewood," said Parker.

When Robyn reached for the ladle in the pot, Parker moved behind her, taking a breath at her neckline. Since they had the same taste in women, Yukon knew his brother would be just as attracted to their guest. He could see it in his eyes too, even if he denied it. For some reason, Yukon didn't have an inkling of jealousy. Not when it came to his brother, anyway.

Since yesterday evening, Parker had started to mellow out, more accepting of their house guest. The atmosphere was more comfortable now that they weren't at each other's throats.

"You want some?" she asked, turning to look up at Parker. They looked like an old married couple, and it nearly made Yukon laugh out loud. It was good having a woman underfoot.

"I ate a couple hours ago. I'm ready to go whenever you are," Parker said.

Yukon's first reaction was to protest, but then he thought better. He hated the rift growing between him and his brother. Spending some time together would be good for both of them. Like the good old days when they had to work as a team. So far, Parker hadn't drank since Robyn showed up, and his mood was improving.

"So you're tagging along?" asked Yukon.

"You might need some muscle." Parker sat down on the chair across for him, nursing his coffee in both hands.

"Well, thanks for that," said Yukon, shaking his head.

Robyn sat at the dinette table in the kitchen. "This is good. I'm not used to eating breakfast," she said. They both turned to look in her direction.

"You don't eat breakfast?" asked Yukon. "It's the most important meal of the day."

Parker nodded in agreement, taking another sip of coffee.

"Well, after getting dressed and doing my make-up, I'm always in a rush to get to the office or court. I usually live on coffee."

"That's no kind of life, darlin'," said Parker.

For once, Yukon was in complete agreement. Rushing around like a chicken with its head cut off was no way to live. She needed time to eat properly and enjoy the little things. City life sounded bad for her health.

"I like to keep busy."

Parker looked at him, the unspoken disapproval passing between them. It was as if they both had the same investment … in the same woman.

"How long can you keep up that pace?" Parker kept pushing, and Yukon was getting nervous that she'd shut herself off again.

"It's not easy. In a few more years, I'll be forty. In my office, that's close to the grave."

Yukon laughed. "Then we're dead and buried, Parker."

"Don't worry," she said. "It's only a concern for women. It's a huge double standard."

"You look perfect the way you are, baby girl." Parker finished his coffee and stood up. As he passed Robyn, he brushed his hand along her shoulder. "If someone doesn't like you for the way you are, you don't need them."

****

Robyn played the words in her head. Not many people accepted her the way she was. In fact, no one knew the real her because she lived to hide her away. Even her closest so-called friends were slowly drifting away because she refused to change herself to fit in with their circles. Yes, the hottest paralegals were assigned the best cases, but she couldn't stay young forever. That deep-seated worry continually bubbled to the surface. It was another reason she liked to keep busy, to avoid too much worry and reflection.

Once they were all ready to go, they rushed through the rain to get to the pick-up truck, and she was sandwiched in the middle of the front bench seat.

"You didn't have to change back into your suit," said Parker. "You'll stick out like a sore thumb."

"I'm not wearing your size-twenty rubber boots, and I don't think heels will look good with Yukon's jogging pants."

"We're not size twenty," Yukon said, his eyes ahead as he drove up the road.

"I don't have my suitcase, so this will have to do. My undies are drying in the bathroom." After she spoke, she regretted telling the brothers there was nothing under her skirt. Her face felt hotter than a furnace, and an awkward silence filled the cab of the truck. These were both virile men, so they had to be imagining all the intimate details.

The more she thought about it, the more she wondered what it would be like to give herself to the two cowboys. Together, they'd make a perfect combination. She'd only had a few sexual encounters in her life, even though her friends thought it was in the dozens. Sometimes she had to lie to fit in, maybe a lot. Most of her image was a sham, and hiding her past a full-time job some days.

"We'll pop over at Ms. Granger's first," said Yukon.

"Who's that?"

"A neighbor. With the power out, I want to be sure she's okay." They stopped the truck in front of a small wooden house. It looked more like a cottage set on acres of open land. "I'll be right back."

It was too quiet. "That's a cute house," she said, once alone with Parker.

"It's one of the century homes. Her husband used to help out our father when we were struggling," said Parker. "Now Ms. Granger's a widow, so we do our best to look out for her."

That was so sweet. Old-fashioned values and neighbors helping neighbors. It was a foreign concept to her. The opposite of the backstabbing she was used to.

"That's really nice of you two."

He shrugged. "Nothing nice about it. In our town, we all look out for each other. It's the cowboy way."

"I'm not from around here, and you're helping me."

Parker leaned into her personal space. He smelled so damn good. "You're a special one," he said. "I usually don't take kindly to strangers."

When his hand came down on her bare thigh, she jerked in her seat.

"Are you cold?"

She shook her head rapidly. If he kept his hand there, so close to her naked pussy, she'd come on the spot.

"You can use my coat like a blanket if you like. Your skin's all broken out into gooseflesh."

He was the reason. It had nothing to do with the

cold. When she saw Yukon heading back to the truck, he was her saving grace. Parker sat up straighter, his hand slipping away.

Yukon's hair was wet, and he gave it a shake before hopping back into the truck. "Everything's okay," he said. "She sends her best."

"She has enough food? Well's working?"

"I checked everything. Mack was by yesterday and topped up her wood pile," said Yukon. "Apparently Laura's going to come visit in a couple months."

It was like she'd fallen asleep and woken up in an episode of *Little House on the Prairie.* Robyn couldn't believe people still acted like this, and cared for each other.

The truck skidded on the slick mud as they left the property and headed back toward their ranch. She braced the edge of the seat with her hands, but both men placed their arms across her at once, keeping her steady. Their protective nature was the ultimate turn on, especially for a woman forced to survive on her own for so long.

"Now what?" she asked.

"Repair work," said Yukon, giving her a wink. That adorable dimple made its appearance. "You can wait in the house until we're done."

"No, I don't like being alone."

"Then you'll stay with us," said Parker.

Yukon parked the truck back at their house, right up close to the barn. Both men opened the whiny metal doors at once, and Parker scooped her up and carried her into the barn like a bride on her wedding day. He rushed her past the bay door and set her on her feet once they were out of the rain.

"You're strong," she whispered. Robyn wasn't a light-weight, but he made her feel like she weighed a hundred pounds.

Suddenly, Yukon was behind her, tucking her moist hair behind her ear. She felt so enveloped, a woman between two mountains ranges. She savored all the sensations, their touch, the scents, and the way they made her feel. Robyn couldn't move, didn't want to do anything but give up control. She was tired of being strong. Putting up a front 24/7 was exhausting.

"She doesn't like to be alone, and we wouldn't want her scared," said Yukon. His touch was mesmerizing. Her eyes briefly fluttering closed.

"We'll keep her close by. I'm sure we'll find a use for her," said Parker.

Her body ignited, her bare pussy pulsing. She squeezed her legs together, convinced they'd know how aroused they made her. The sound of the rain on the barn roof relaxed her, made her drift into a fantasy-like state. Yukon continued to pet her hair, Parker's hand running down her arm until their fingers touched.

"I have a milking bench you can sit on." Yukon walked off, giving her a bit of reprieve.

Parker tilted her chin up. "Your pupils are dilated." He ran the pad of his thumb along her lower lip, and she nearly opened her mouth for him.

"It's dark in here."

"If you say so." He left her standing alone. Craving more.

Once she was sitting on the wooden bench near the open side doors, she watched the brothers at work from her sheltered seat. A huge oak had crashed down from the storm, luckily over one of their fences rather than the barn. They said it had to be mended or wild hogs and other wildlife would destroy their unharvested crops. She knew so little about their lifestyle, but she started to feel like she belonged. A few times she'd stop and realize that she wasn't obsessing over getting home or worrying about tomorrow. This place had created a bubble of time and space that she was becoming lost in—maybe never to return. Who would miss her?

Robyn had fairy tale sickness, and as far as she knew, there was no cure.

Time passed slowly, comfortably.

She heard a snort, and looked to the other end of the barn. Robyn got up to investigate and discovered two horses—one brown, one black. She'd never been around farm animals, even though she thought horses were beautiful in pictures. They were huge. She hesitantly reached out and rubbed the nose of the black one. It felt softer than silk. Robyn smiled as she searched for something to feed him, grabbing a handful of hay from nearby. The beast was surprisingly calm, with big, expressive eyes. She continued to pet both for a while before returning to the bench.

Watching the brothers' hard bodies working in the rain was addicting. The smell of barley hay was decidedly soothing. Just because her parents had come from a small town didn't make all small towns bad. She saw that now, saw there were still good people outside the city. Robyn's parents had abandoned her as a baby, left her wrapped only in a bloodied t-shirt—but that wasn't her fault. The countless foster homes, the abuse, the sadness … it was all part of her story, and it couldn't be undone. She had to get over her hang-ups, but it was hard to make an overnight change. Her insecurities ran deep.

"Shit!"

Her attention was diverted back to the brothers. Yukon was on the ground and Parker stood over him. She ran out to them, not caring about the rain or her only dry clothes. "What happened?"

"There was some old barbed wire. It got snaked around Yukon's leg."

She looked down and saw the rain dripping red. "Get it off him!" she shouted.

"I'm trying."

Yukon barely winced, leaning up on his elbows as his brother used a pair of pliers to free him, one barb at a time. When he'd gotten the wire out of the way, Yukon pulled himself up onto his good leg. Robyn wrapped her arms around his side. "Are you okay?"

"Just a cut, baby girl. I'll be fine."

"I'm going to finish closing up the fence, get inside for now," said Parker, the rain rushing over his face as he spoke.

They entered the barn, and she forced Yukon to sit on her bench.

"You're soaked to the skin," he said, looking up at her.

Her suit was indeed sopping wet, her blouse clinging to her breasts, leaving little to the imagination. Yukon wasn't even trying to hide the fact he was staring.

"Let me see your leg." She squatted down and tugged off his big boot. Blood dripped down his pant leg. "Ugh. Take your pants off."

"You sure about that?"

She ignored his teasing and motioned for him to lose the pants. He stood up over her, unbuckling his thick leather belt. As he unzipped, she swallowed hard. She tried to avert her gaze, but couldn't stop staring. His black boxer briefs barely hid the massive erection sported diagonally over his thigh. The man was hung like a damn horse. It was unreal. Was she still staring?

"How's it look?" he asked once he'd tossed his pants.

She gasped and looked up at him from her low

crouch.

"The leg…"

"Right." She took a breath and focused on the bloody tear that zigzagged around his leg, just above his knee. "It looks bad." Robyn was no doctor. All she could think to suggest was getting it clean and adding Polysporin.

"Think you can bandage it up for me later?"

"Sure. I'll try my best," she said.

Parker came in the barn, his breathing heavy. "It'll hold for now. We can finish up once this damn rain stops." He pulled off his wet shirt, the material dropping heavily to the ground. Her hormones were on overdrive with the two half-naked cowboys crowding her. They were so wet, so tempting. They smelled like musky cologne and fresh rain.

"Do you have bandages in the house?" she asked.

Parker bent down at look at Yukon's leg, clapping him hard in the shoulder as he stood. "He'll live. Just a little scratch." He winked at his brother.

As they were about to leave the barn, the clouds decided to drop rain by the bucketful. They'd have to wait it out a bit. She could hardly see the house from the static of the rain and mist.

"Come on," said Parker. He took one of her hands, and Yukon grabbed the other, then the three of them darted across the lot toward the house. She couldn't stop laughing. It was like being a kid, carefree, and happy. Her childhood had been something she wanted to forget, but this was perfect. She never wanted the day to end.

By the time they burst into the house, they were all soaked and laughing. "You two are nuts," she said. "Look at us!"

They were all filthy, sprayed by mud, and

sopping wet.

Parker braced an arm on the closed door, trapping her from entering farther. "Take it all off. We wouldn't want to wet the hardwood, now would we?"

He was playing a dangerous game, because right now she wanted to be naked and under both men. Which was ridiculous.

She dared to wrap her hand around his belt buckle, daring him with her eyes. "You're wet, too."

"Let her be," said Yukon, giving his brother a casual shove. "I'm injured, remember?"

"Stop being a baby." Parker continued to stare at her, but she slipped under his arm.

"I'll get changed, then I'll take care of Yukon."

Chapter Ten

Parker watched Robyn rush upstairs. She was driving him nuts, making him feel like he was twenty again. "Have you ever seen a nicer ass?"

"She sure fills a skirt the way God intended," said Yukon.

They were both hard up for the same woman. She'd probably leave them both in the blink of an eye once the storm passed. But, like his brother, Parker still couldn't keep his distance. He kept telling himself it was flirting, trying to see how far he could get. The truth was he was falling for her. He was an idiot, some kind of sick masochist.

Parker had to keep himself from crossing the line or Yukon would never forgive him. He'd been warning his brother, but fell for the same temptation. It didn't help that she knew exactly how to push his buttons.

"Okay, that's better," she said once she hit the bottom step. Her hair was up in a loose bun, showcasing her heart-shaped face. She was back in Yukon's sweats. Likely without panties. "Why haven't either of you changed?"

Only then did he realize they were both standing there, dripping on the floor. His mind was a mess, and his balls ached. Yukon looked just as love-struck.

"Later," said Parker. "Worry about Yukon for now." He opened the cabinet in the kitchen where they kept their medical kit. It was well used by both of them. Over the years, they'd been in countless minor and serious scrapes. Doctors cost money, so they tried to mend themselves when they could.

Yukon was in just his boxers. He sat on the end of the couch, with his leg up over the cushions. Robyn sat on the coffee table and taped a gauze dipped in alcohol over the cuts. Yukon cringed, and Parker snorted. He couldn't help it. Their little nurse didn't have a clue what she was doing, but she was damn cute trying.

"You're not a very nice brother, you know," Robyn said.

"I'm just teasing," said Parker. "Yukon knows how much I love him."

He leaned back in the chair, watching the elegant line of Robyn's neck. His mouth salivated.

"I can't believe you're both living in this big, old house all alone," she said. "Well, at least you have each other."

"It's not the same," said Yukon. "Even God said man shouldn't be alone. Maybe he forgot about us."

"Don't say that," she said. "There's someone for everyone." They were all quiet while she did her nursing. When she finished, she tidied up the medical kit. "Good as new."

Yukon had that look again, the one he'd only worn since Robyn showed up in their town. "It's nice to be mothered. I can hardly remember our mother now. If I didn't have a picture, I'd forget her face."

"You remember," said Parker. "Her eyes were so blue in the sunlight. Just like yours. Remember how she used to sing when she'd cook dinner?"

"Oh yeah, I remember." Yukon smiled to himself.

Parker didn't talk much about it, forever trying to be the stronger one for the sake of Yukon, but the death of his parents had hit him hard. He wanted to have a mother dote over him, and a father to keep him in line. But, in the blink of an eye, they were gone. A memory.

"How about you, Robyn? Your parents living?"

She bit her bottom lip, and began to fiddle with the kit again. "I'm not sure."

"What do you mean?" asked Yukon.

Robyn stood up, tucking the kit under one arm. "I don't really have contact. We weren't close or anything."

Parker narrowed his eyes, trying to figure her out. He followed her to the kitchen, taking the kit from her and setting it back in the high cupboard. "Don't keep secrets, little one. I'm not here to judge you."

She exhaled and looked up at him. There was such vulnerability in her eyes. "I was put into foster care when I was a baby. I've never had parents."

"You weren't adopted?"

Robyn shook her head. "Guess I was an ugly baby." She tried to joke, but he wasn't buying it. "I've been on my own a long time. I don't need anyone but myself."

Poor thing felt unwanted, rejected. It shaped her right down to the core. It explained a fucking lot. Any resentment he had for her fizzled away, leaving only the desire to be what she needed. How could he heal a broken woman?

"You don't have to be alone," he said.

"I'm used to it," she said. "It doesn't bother me."

He wanted to push her to be honest with herself. It would help her to get rid of that baggage. But tonight, he'd leave her be. He didn't want to press too hard and sound like an asshole.

Parker wanted to tell her she needed a good man to take care of her, but maybe she equated that care to luxuries only money could buy. He was getting a fucking complex, wanting to be everything for her, but not sure it would ever be enough.

"How about some hot cocoa? It'll warm us up." When she nodded in agreement, she had the innocent air of a little girl. How could her parents give up such an angel? He wanted to protect her from the world. He instinctively kissed her on the temple, shocked by the new emotions taking him by storm. "I'll bring it to you in a few minutes. Go check on your patient."

His mind was on overdrive. Yukon wanted Robyn, but so did he. He wanted to share her with his brother, but who the hell would agree to that? If she decided country life was for her, he'd step aside for his brother.

****

Robyn hoped the topic never came up again. Her embarrassment was on overdrive. She hated exposing the truth about her past. It revealed her vulnerabilities, made people look at her differently, like she was damaged goods.

After dinner that night, they sat in front of the fire on a series of old patchwork rugs. It was so simple and peaceful. The flames roared: red, orange, yellow. The wood smelled sweet and earthly. Yukon said it was from an old apple tree.

It was hard to believe there was a world beyond this town, a city, a courtroom, a million people rushing around, forgetting how to live. The brothers were right, she'd been blind to the simple pleasures just because of her own insecurities.

She felt comfortable with Yukon and Parker, no fear, no expectations. Back home, it was always about appearances, creating the right image. She hadn't worn make-up since showing up on their doorstep, or bothered to put on an act. It was refreshing to just be herself.

"You have a tattoo," she said. Parker stretched out on his side, exposing the scrollwork on his inner arm. She'd always been curious, but it seemed like a good time to ask. "What's it say?"

Parker glanced at his arm. "It's nothing."

"What's it say?" she insisted.

He shook his head. "Don't matter."

Her curiosity soared.

"Just show her," said Yukon with a chuckle. "He got it when he was twenty-two. Young and stupid."

Robyn leaned over and reached for his arm, but Parker continued to pull away. She toppled over and they began wrestling on the rugs like two kids. He tickled her sides until she was a ball of laughter. Yukon joined in, and soon there were hands all over her. She fought to catch her breath, kicking and squealing. The heat of the fire soothed her bare skin as her shirt lifted a few inches, exposing her bare stomach.

"Stop!" she shouted. Robyn needed to breathe. She'd never realized she was ticklish, but now knew she had a major weakness they could exploit. "Please."

She lay on the carpets, looking up at both men as they leaned over her, her breathing labored. Robyn traced a finger along Yukon's jaw line, resting her hand on Parker's bicep. God, she actually falling in love with two men. The thought of leaving terrified her. She'd found that fairy tale place, that little piece of heaven made just for her—it had to be too good to be true. Shelly insisted happily ever afters didn't exist.

"Take off your shirt," she said, looking at Parker. He complied immediately, revealing his chiseled torso. She ran her hand from the corded muscle in his shoulder, down his arm … to the tattoo. When she tried to peek at the wording, he grabbed her waist and rolled her above him.

"Oh, no you don't," he said.

His belt buckle rubbed against her pussy as she straddled his body, so she shifted down slightly—right into his erection. His dick pressed tight to her most intimate parts, throbbing against her pussy and ass. She pretended not to notice to save them both embarrassment, but she didn't dare move away. It felt too good. His hard, virile cock was only a thin layer of denim away, and her mouth salivated when her imagination took over.

"Just show her," said Yukon, flopping down on his side next to them. Could they feel the sexual tension in the air? It was practically suffocating her. Their innocent games were anything but, and she only craved more.

"Please." She braced her weight on his shoulders, loving the feel of his warm skin. "Arms up."

"First, you have do something for me," said Parker.

"Okay."

"Give Yukon a kiss, then I'll show you."

Everyone shut up after he spoke, and the entire world seemed to stop. Her pussy tingled, and she swore she'd combust on the spot. Why wouldn't he ask for his own kiss? His body obviously wanted a lot more than first base.

She knew Parker loved Yukon. Their connection and love was palpable, even when they fought. Parker had tried to protect his brother from heartache since day one, so maybe he was trying to pave the way for Yukon. Did he trust her not to break his brother's heart now? It was the weirdest situation she'd ever been caught in, but it was oddly titillating.

Yukon sat up, getting to his knees. Fuck, he was gorgeous. He cupped her face with one hand, not even questioning Parker. "You taking him up on his offer?"

She nodded without thinking. *Stupid, stupid.*

With Parker still between her legs, she leaned to the side and kissed Yukon on the lips. It was her choice. They never pushed her, never demanded anything. She intended to give him a quick peck to keep her end of the deal, but she couldn't stop there. The kiss morphed into something more, something monumental. His tongue begged for entrance and she opened for him, kissing him back with all the passion she felt. If she didn't stop now, she'd be fucking both men on the floor by the fire. But she couldn't stop. She felt dirty and wanton, her sexuality breaking free for the first time in her life.

A loud bang stole Yukon's attention.

Both men were off the ground within seconds, heading to the front door. She followed along to see what was going on. Maybe it was some kind of rescue or police update on the situation.

Once Parker wrenched open the door, she saw a soaking wet man standing in the darkness. "My car's in the ditch half a mile up the road. Do you have a phone I can use?"

"Phone lines are down from the storm," said Parker.

"Do you mind if I stay until morning? I'd stay in my car, but it's a write-off."

The brothers looked at each other for a moment, but said nothing.

"You can have the couch for tonight. Our spare room's already taken," said Yukon.

"You guys are a life saver." He looked to be in his early thirties, with a baseball cap and nylon jacket. He stepped inside and took off his hat, scrubbing a hand over his face. "It's wicked out there."

"You're not from around here," said Yukon.

The man chuckled. "You know everyone in the town?"

"Yeah, I do. Where you heading, stranger?"

"I was driving up to the rodeo, got free tickets from work. My name's Ed, by the way."

Yukon kept assessing him. "There's stew in the kitchen, if you're hungry. Bowls are in the cupboard."

"Great. Thanks. Is there a bathroom nearby?"

"Just the one. Very top of the stairs," said Yukon.

The entire time, Parker had his hand casually on the butt end of a rifle near the door. He looked even more displeased with their guest than Yukon, which said a lot. At least they hadn't thrown him back into the storm. What harm could he do against the two hulking cowboys?

Disappointment assaulted her. What if that man hadn't shown up? How far would the brothers have taken things? Did she even want to know?

Parker still hadn't shown her his tattoo, but she'd kept her end of the deal.

Yukon approached her once the stranger sat on the sofa. He was right in her personal space, leaning over to speak in her ear. She had to hold back her urge to touch him, to rest her hand on his chest. "It's late. We should get to bed, eh?"

She nodded. The guy on the sofa stared at her. He gave her the creeps.

"Okay, I'll see you in the morning." She wondered where things stood now. Would he kiss her goodnight? Had it all been part of their game?

Chapter Eleven

Yukon didn't trust strangers. He'd heard all about the looting down south when families were forced from their homes due to the storm system. There were always assholes ready to take advantage of another person's kindness. Was this man genuinely in trouble or had he been looking for an easy target? He wasn't from town, because if he had been, they would have welcomed him inside with open arms.

He was more irritated than anything. His intimate time with Robyn had been cut short thanks to this stranger. He'd been deep in the best kiss of his life when the man knocked on the door. Things were finally looking up for him, and he hoped what they shared hadn't been one-sided.

That evening, Parker turned off the generator to give it a rest. They had lanterns ready around the house. Yukon took a drink of water in the kitchen, watching the moon's glow from behind the clouds from the window. The storm was clearing, and that meant his chances with Robyn were thin to none. She'd want a ride out first thing in the morning. Unless the kiss meant something to her too.

He put his glass in the sink. Yukon should have been happy they hadn't taken on the same damage as the farms down south. It was a blessing. Then why did he feel so shitty?

Before heading upstairs to bed, he ensured the stranger, Ed, was sleeping on the sofa. He didn't like the idea having the man in their home, especially with Robyn under the roof.

A strip of light shined under Parker's bedroom door, but Yukon was in no mood to hear his brother's negativity. He went to his room and sat on the edge of the bed.

He still remembered when he'd first seen Robyn at Meg's. There'd been instant attraction, and he knew she was the one. Only, she'd hated him then, but he hoped she saw something worthwhile in him now. He had no time to entice her, to show her the man under the skin. He needed more than a few days to court a woman properly.

Yukon was more than a struggling cowboy. He had hopes and dreams, and knew he'd give his woman all he had. But there was no time to prove a thing to Robyn, and besides, Parker was probably right. She likely wanted a man in a suit with a heavy wallet.

He took a deep breath and dropped back on his bed. Knowing she was on the other side of his bedroom wall put him in an uncomfortable predicament. He was sure the city boys couldn't rock her in bed the way he could. Yukon wasn't afraid to get dirty, to give her every kind of wicked pleasure. He ran a hand over his jeans, his cock aching for attention.

He slowly began to fall asleep, his daydreams of Robyn pulling him out of reality.

When he heard a creak in the hall, he bolted back up into a sitting position, his faculties rushing back as he focused on the sound.

He stood up and moved closer to the door. It was late, no lights to illuminate his room or the hallway. Only the faint glow of the moon allowed him to see shadows. The sound of a door creaking open was the final straw. He opened his bedroom door and looked down the hallway, noticing a dark figure enter Robyn's room. It could be Parker, but it could also be Ed.

Yukon moved quietly, knowing exactly where to step to keep on the down low. When he peered in

Robyn's room, he knew the man wasn't his brother.
Parker was his size, well over six feet, and Ed had a
much smaller frame.

"Lost?" he asked, keeping his voice low.

The shadow whirled around. "Oh, shit. I thought
this was the bathroom."

"Did you now? It's still at the top of the stairs.
Hasn't moved."

Ed walked toward the door, his arms outstretched.
"I get disoriented in the dark."

When he tried to move past him, Yukon braced
his arm out to the side. "Close the door. Quietly."

Ed did as told.

"I don't take kindly to a stranger in my woman's
room. Makes me ... uncomfortable." He didn't hide the
threat in his voice.

"I didn't know you were together."

"Now you know."

"I'll get my ass downstairs. I won't be any more
trouble."

He grabbed the scruff of Ed's shirt, nearly lifting
him off his feet. Yukon whispered in his ear. "Once first
light comes, I want you gone. If you come up these stairs
again tonight, I'll fucking kill you." After a shove, he
waited until Ed was downstairs. The little shit didn't
protest or try to argue his innocence. Yukon was no fool.
That man wanted a piece of Robyn.

Yukon would have tossed him out in the dead of
night, but he knew Robyn would be safe because he'd be
sleeping in her room. It was the only way to ensure Ed
didn't try to creep into her bed later in the night.

He opened her door, closing it behind him. Once
his eyes adjusted, the moonlight from her window aided
him in seeing which side of the bed she slept on. He
carefully sat down on the opposite side and brought his

legs up on the bed, settling on the extra pillow. Yukon took a breath. *What was I thinking?* He wouldn't get any sleep tonight, not with Robyn less than a foot from him. Her scent was sweet and subtle, enough to arouse him. In fact, everything about their guest drove him crazy—from her dark eyes to those rounded hips. It was more than her looks, though. Vulnerability surrounded her. She had a quiet soul in need of healing. He was tired of the loud-mouthed farmer's daughters. Girls without substance.

He wanted to be everything she needed.

Yukon closed his eyes, imagining a life with Robyn. He wasn't a young man anymore. He was more than ready to settle down at this point in his life. His father had taught him an important lesson—growing old alone could break a man.

The mattress shifted as she moved. "Yukon?" she whispered.

"Don't worry, darling. I'm not trying anything funny."

"I know. I heard."

"You all right with me sleeping here? I have all my clothes on," he said. "I don't trust that drifter."

"It's okay." She turned to her side, facing him. The room was too quiet. Even the static of the rain on their tin roof had silenced. "Thanks for taking care of me."

"You're my guest. It's my job to take care of you."

She stayed quiet for a minute. "Parker thinks it may be more than that."

"What do you mean?"

"He said that you liked me. Is that true?"

Yukon couldn't wait to get his hands on his brother. Why the fuck would he say such a stupid thing to Robyn? He was lucky he hadn't scared her off.

"Parker has a big mouth."

"So, it's not true?"

What should he say? Tell her Parker was a liar? Embarrass himself by telling the truth?

"You know I like you. I bought you a drink at Meg's Longhorn, remember?"

"I remember." She reached out, her hand resting on his bicep. His entire body went stiff. "It's hard to believe you'd be interested in my type."

"Why wouldn't I?" He turned his head. "I'm a man. You're a beautiful woman. It's only natural."

"I usually expect the worst from everyone."

"That's what city living will do to you," he said.

"It's all I know. I'm trying to make something of myself."

"In what way? Around here the end goal is usually a family, not fame and fortune."

****

Robyn had yet to fall asleep. It was the same drill, the anxiety of sleeping in a strange bed. There'd been so many, each with its own story she wanted to forget. She'd tossed and turned, her fears and weaknesses making themselves painfully known. Then that guy tried to sneak in her room. It was like her childhood nightmares all over again.

When Yukon took charge, it sparked something deep inside her. He'd protected her, saved her from her demons. She realized what a bitch she'd been by keeping her distance. Robyn had been judging him based on his social status when she'd come from the very bottom herself. Lower than anyone.

Now, Yukon was in her bed, and the cascade of relief sparked new desires. She didn't want to be alone, not now or ever. She kept trying to convince herself a good man, a cowboy like Yukon wasn't in the cards for her. All her adult life, she'd wanted a man with power, money, and influence. She wanted to create herself into something better, something strong and indestructible. A woman worth respect. A woman who mattered.

Her ideals were crashing down around her.

"Where I'm from, success in business ranks higher than starting a family."

"Sounds sad, but then again, I'm living alone with my brother." He chuckled, the deep sound a comfort in the darkness.

She wanted Yukon, wanted to feel his strong hands all over her body. To feel his lips again. He'd never break her heart, never cast her aside. She didn't want him to play the gentleman another minute. His huge frame dipped the bed, his musky scent making her pussy tingle. She wanted all his clothes off, wanted to know what it felt like to be dominated by a cowboy.

"Why are you both alone? I mean, if family's so important to you?" she asked.

"I don't want just any woman."

He moved onto his side, and she could feel the weight of his stare even in the dark.

"What's your type?"

"*You're* my type."

She swallowed hard, her heartbeat pounding in her ears. Yes, she'd fucked around with men in her life—businessmen, men with degrees and big wallets—but not one of them made her feel like a woman in love.

Robyn painted a fingertip down his chest, wishing it was his bare skin under her touch. When had things changed? Or was it her? She'd sworn never to settle for a working-class man. Rising to the top had been her life's mission. Now she just wanted to fall into the strong arms of a cowboy—one with calloused hands and the bluest eyes.

"You're holding back," he said, still playing the gentleman. His control was starting to piss her off. A sexual tsunami was playing out inside her body, and it took all her resolve to wait for his next move.

Robyn shook her head. "I'm just playing the part," she said. "Don't country girls mind their manners?"

"But you're a city girl, darlin'. And I'm not interested in any one else." The mattress tilted as he pushed up on one arm, moving into her space. He leaned down and nuzzled her neck. The scent of sandalwood titillated her senses.

She exhaled as he kissed behind her ear, his tongue slowly shelling the rim. The man was more skilled than she imagined possible. Most men wanted a quick fuck and a "get out of a relationship" card the next morning. Yukon was something different. She had a feeling he'd show her what it felt like to be worshiped by a man.

"What are you hiding?" he whispered in her ear. His lips grazed her cheek, his free hand skimming down her side. She only wore an oversized t-shirt and panties. When his fingers slipped under the bottom edge of her shirt, he ran his hand over the swell of her lower stomach … then higher. Robyn gasped when his big, rough hand cupped her bare breast. Her nipples were already hard and achy, so the simple touch sent shivers skittering all the way to her clit.

"You have soft skin." He inched his way closer to her lips, his coarse stubble arousing her in new, indecent ways. When he kissed her, she closed her eyes, heat lashing out all the way to her extremities. Every move he made was slow, sensual, controlled. The kiss was soft and gentle, but soon became all-encompassing. She'd never known passion until today. Robyn felt completely dominated, branded, and claimed—and they hadn't even past first base.

Their tongues played a sensual game, Yukon's hulking frame pressing harder against her by the minute. Things escalated quickly, their mutual desire spiraling out of control. She couldn't kiss and touch him enough.

"Take this off," she said between kisses, tugging at his flannel shirt. He complied without hesitation, sitting up on his knees and yanking off the shirt without unbuttoning it. Only a hint of moonlight cast into the guest room, enough to highlight the hard planes of his muscles. God, she wanted him.

She reached up, beckoning him to lower his body over hers. She needed him more than breath. He unbuckled his belt, the metal clang and whip of leather followed by a zipper lowering. Yukon dropped down, supporting his weight on his strong arms. She felt completely enveloped by his presence and male heat.

"You drive me crazy," he said. "From the moment I saw you, I knew you'd be mine."

They kissed and explored each other's bodies. He reached down the front of her panties, his hand cupping her pussy. She arched up into his touch, needing more. "Yukon…"

"So ripe." He slipped two fingers into her pussy, pushing all the way in to his knuckles. She mewled and stirred beneath him. He moved his fingers in just the right way, enough to leave her hanging desperately on a precipice. "You want more, baby?"

"Yes."

"Such a hot little cunt." Yukon took his fingers away, leaving her wanting. He kicked off his jeans and removed all her clothing. They were both naked, exposed, both ready to go all the way. He was such a tempting mix of nice and naughty.

When he lowered over her, she smoothed her hands all over his hard back, unable to get enough of him. He didn't have an ounce of fat, just homegrown muscle on muscle. "Give it to me," she said, beyond caring what she sounded like. She felt more animal than woman.

"I'm all yours." He slid the head of his cock up and down her slit. Her pussy was already soaking, had been since he lay down on her bed. When he pushed the tip of his cock past her entrance, she gasped at his size. She remembered her conversations with Shelly about dick size, and this cowboy would take the first-place trophy. "Relax for me, sweet thing," he said.

The man knew he was huge, likely experienced on taking his time with women. She didn't want to play nice. She wanted it all, every inch of him.

He kept working her body, easing inside her, teasing her erogenous zones with his tongue. Once fully inside her, he hooked his arms under her shoulders and gave a final push, confirming she'd taken every inch. He growled his approval, and she could feel the pulse of his cock inside her. She'd never felt so full and satisfied in her life, and he hadn't even started.

"You okay?" he asked.

She pulled his neck down and kissed his lips, giving him a little nip. "I've never been with a cowboy."

"You don't know what you've been missing."

They devoured each other. He began to pump into her, no cell inside her left untouched. She wrapped her legs around his hips, urging him for more. He was a machine, fucking her with the stamina of a stud horse. It amazed her, being with such a capable lover.

Within minutes, the old wooden bed was creaking, the headboard knocking against the wall. She didn't care. Actually, she didn't care about anything—

not yesterday or tomorrow—so unlike her. All that mattered was Yukon and his skills beneath the blankets.

****

Yukon had wanted to play the gentleman but knew he also had limited time to win Robyn over. Once she put her little hands on him, all bets were off. He could practically feel her desire, her need, and he wasn't going to deny her.

He loved everything about her body, and he wanted to explore every soft curve. Yukon needed a woman with strong hips and tits that overflowed in his hands. He'd been pent up since he'd first set eyes on her, so it took all his resolve not to ram into her from the starting gate. Instead, he eased into her pussy with all the patience he could muster. His city girl was hot and tight, hugging his cock like a glove. Her kisses were addicting, so much more than any woman he'd fucked around with. He wanted to own her, to be her man. Yukon wasn't rich, but he'd show her that cowboys could outbest any educated man in bed and beyond.

"I love fucking you," he said between breaths. Robyn was a minx, prodding him with her heels, arching to meet him thrust for thrust. Parker was right, the quiet ones were the wildest in the bedroom.

The bed nearly shattered into splinters. He pistoned in and out of her cunt, his cock never so hard and eager. He swore he could go all night long. When she began to tremble, he reached between them to tease her clit.

"I'm going to come," she said, seeking his lips again. He couldn't deny her a thing. Her kisses went deeper than lust. He could feel her need and vulnerability mixed with the passion.

Parker was wrong. They were meant for each other.

As her body convulsed with an orgasm, he rammed her hard, filling her to overflowing. He helped her ride out the waves, savoring the sound of her squeals and feminine moans. Only when he knew she was fully sated did he allow himself to let go.

His release was intense, pulsing on and on as he filled her with his seed. He dropped to the side, pulling her with him, his cock still deep inside her. The only sound in the room was their heavy breathing.

"That was perfect," he said. Yukon ran his hand through her hair, getting the moistened hairs off her face. "How do you feel about cowboys now?"

She smirked but didn't say anything. Robyn shifted more comfortably into his embrace, resting her head on his shoulder. As she fell asleep in his arms, he knew she'd stolen his heart.

Chapter Twelve

After a fitful night's sleep, Parker woke up with a start. Sunlight beamed through the cracks in his curtains, signaling the worst of the storm was gone.

He rubbed his hand over his morning wood. It had been torture listening to Robyn's little mewling sounds while Yukon fucked her down the hall. He'd gone to investigate when he'd heard banging in the old guest room. It only took a minute for him to realize exactly what was going on. Yukon was getting lucky with the city girl. It would only be worse for him now when she walked out of his life. But, fuck, he'd warned him numerous times.

He sat up in bed and scrubbed a hand over his face. That was when he heard the knocking on the main door. Parker pulled on a pair of jeans and bounded down the stairs. With the worst of the weather past, he'd have to get back to work. Everything could get back to normal, in addition to any damage control around the property.

Parker expected that little prick was back. He had thrown Ed out first thing in the morning when he went to check on the horses. He knew what went down the night before, and didn't want him near Robyn today.

Before he hit the bottom step, Yukon was behind him. This would be the third unexpected visit in the last couple days. Something neither of them were used to. They were accustomed to their solitary life, one where everyone chose to keep away.

"Ed?"

"Long gone," said Parker.

"Now what?"

"Guess we'll find out." Parker would wait until

later to grill his brother about his night with Robyn. Little Miss Proper should have been in his bed, but he'd pushed her away for the sake of Yukon. If it wasn't for Ed, maybe the three of them would have spent the night together by the fire. He'd never know what could have been.

Parker opened the door once his brother had a shotgun in hand. Standing on the other side of the door was a hot number in a long coat with a fancy-ass businessman carrying a briefcase. What in God's name was going on? They didn't ask for any of this damn attention.

"Can I help you?" he asked.

"I know Robyn's in there. The woman at the diner sent us to this address," said the blonde.

"Maybe she is, maybe she isn't. Who the hell are you?" asked Parker.

She looked him less than discreetly up and down. They were both in their blue jeans and nothing more. Their visitor was lucky they'd put on that much, considering the early hour.

"I work with her. We were separated because of the storm. Do I need to get the police involved?"

"Sugar, do whatever the fuck you like."

He crossed his arms over his chest. Yes, he'd wanted Robyn gone, knew she'd be a problem in their lives. But now, faced with the fact she'd soon be whisked away to the city, his hackles were up. A new territorial anger building up inside him.

"Shelly?"

Parker and Yukon turned at the same time. Robyn rushed over from the staircase, wearing one of their t-shirts.

Shelly pushed past them without apology and rushed toward Robyn. They embraced in the middle of the living room. "I'm so sorry, Robyn. Oh God, you have no idea how sorry I am."

"Where the fuck were you? I've been stuck here for days."

"Long story," said Shelly. "But we're here now. I have your stuff in the car, so you'll be all set."

"For what?"

"We got the papers signed this morning with Marla Winters. Now we have to head to a bigger town just north of here. We'll be there about a week."

Robyn shook her head. "No more. Look at me. I just want to go home. I never signed up for this shit."

"Look around, I don't see any Ubers waiting to take you back to the city. Calloway's already pissed this deal is taking so long, storm or no storm."

"Where've you been staying?"

Parker could feel Robyn's anger and frustration. Her so-called friend had left to fend for herself. If Yukon hadn't found her, she could have had a much different experience. When cowboys and drifters started drinking at night, bad shit happened.

"It doesn't look like you've been too hard up," Shelly said, turning to look at him and his brother. "You're welcome."

Robyn's hands balled into fists. "Are you joking? This isn't funny. I could have been dead for all you knew."

Shelly shrugged. "Look, I'm sorry. Let's get the hell out of here."

The guy at the door stepped in. "Do you have anything I can carry?" he asked.

"No, I didn't even have my purse. I came here with the clothes on my back." Robyn practically spat the words. She looked hot when she was pissed off.

"I have a nice room reserved. You'll love it," said

the asshole.

"Who the fuck are you?" asked Yukon.

The man took a step back. He was a fancy boy with manicured nails and salon hair. Probably hadn't worked a man's day in his life. Yukon towered over him.

"Peter Brighton. I'm working this case with Robyn and Shelly." He reached out a hand, but Yukon only palmed his rifle.

"Robyn has a *nice* room here."

Peter was smart and kept his mouth shut.

"I'll get my clothes." Robyn went back upstairs. Parker followed her.

He stood in the bedroom doorway as she bent down to pick up one of her things off the floor. When she turned and saw him, she froze.

"Time to run away?" he asked. "I knew you'd break my brother's heart."

"Just stop, please."

"I heard you two fucking last night. You thought that would help? I asked you to keep your distance, but apparently that was too much to ask," he said.

"I don't have a choice. It's my job. I'll get fired if I don't go." She rushed around the room, collecting her things. "Besides, this was temporary. It's not like anything can actually work with me and your brother. We're from two different worlds."

"That's right, you're more interested in men with high-priced degrees, no? Like the prick downstairs?"

"He's not a prick. He's a well-respected lawyer."

"And your friend?"

She turned to look at him. "Where I'm from, it's the best I'll get."

He narrowed his eyes. "You should have a higher bar for yourself, darlin'. You're letting the world take you for a real shit ride."

Once her arms were full, she approached the doorway. "Thank you for letting me stay. I'm sorry if I was any trouble."

Something happened between all of them yesterday. He thought she'd changed, but he was wrong.

He wouldn't let her pass. As much as he kept telling himself he was protecting Yukon, he was protecting himself, too. He liked her. Too much. A small part of him hoped she was different from other city girls, but he was a fool in love. Women from the city were narrowed-minded, lovers of money, and ready to cast people aside.

"It's that simple, is it? Just keep running without looking back?"

"Nothing's simple," she said.

When she looked up at him, he saw the conflict in her eyes.

"Kiss me," he said.

"What?"

"A goodbye kiss, then you can leave. No hard feelings."

"Fine."

He took a step into the room, cupping her face into his hands. "You can run all you want, but you'll be running forever. No man will love you like Yukon. Remember that when you're back in your real world." No man would love her like *him*.

Parker bent down and kissed her on the lips. He'd been fantasizing about the softness of her kiss. She dropped her clothes and placed her hands on his chest, kissing him back. If only things were different, but they couldn't be more complicated.

He pulled away. "About that tattoo. It says *Courage is being scared to death ... and saddling up anyway.* I got the old Western bug from our dad. Seemed appropriate when I was riding bulls." Parker moved to the side and opened his arm, inviting her to leave. "I'll see you around."

****

Robyn hadn't expected Shelly to show up first thing in the morning—or ever. She expected to have more time to think, to decide what to do. She'd spent the hottest night of her life with Yukon, and he'd made it clear he wanted more than one night. The whole idea of commitment and security terrified her. It was out of her element, and real happiness just wasn't meant for her. Sure, she'd tried to conform and fit in, but it was all an act. Real happiness was different, something unattainable for most people she knew, including her. That was what drugs and alcohol were for—getting through life with as little reflection as possible.

Parker stepped aside. He had the body of a god, his Wranglers low on his etched hips. His kiss confused her. So did his words.

She had to leave before she lost her mind … and her heart.

"I'm ready," she said once downstairs again. Robyn needed to get out of this house. Seeing Shelly and Peter in the flesh brought back reality. Her stay with the brothers was a dream, a fantasy, and it was time to get back to real life.

She thrust her clothes in Shelly's arms and her friend left the house with Peter. *Friend* was being used very loosely at this point. It seemed everyone in Robyn's life would trade her for as little as a custom latte. Shelly chose sex with a lawyer over their friendship, but Robyn had to suck it up, internalize it, and play like nothing mattered. That was what she was good at.

"You're leaving?" Yukon ran a hand through his tousled hair, betrayal in his blue eyes. She wanted to touch him, to throw herself into his strong, capable arms, but that wouldn't help. Robyn had to be strong, had to close off her emotions if she wanted to survive the next couple hours.

"It's just work. I have to finish this assignment."

"And then what?"

She shrugged. "Then I go home, I guess."

"Baby, I want you here. With me," said Yukon. "Tell me what you want and I'll give it to you."

"Let her go," said Parker, approaching them. "It's time for our guest to get back to her real life. You can't force someone to love you."

"I'm sorry," she said, then she rushed out the door.

She jogged up the drive to Shelly's SUV and slammed the door shut. "Let's go. Hurry, please."

Peter laughed. "She really wants to get away from here. What did those two heathens do to you?"

"Nothing. I just want to forget any of this ever happened."

Yukon's words kept playing in her head. He wanted her to stay—permanently. Another woman may be thrilled at the prospect of having a gorgeous, attentive man ready to commit. She believed him, too. The man was like an open book, his emotions hard to misunderstand. He'd be a great husband—patient, devoted, and amazing in bed.

That was why she was running. It was too good to be true. Bound to come crashing down around her. And she couldn't commit to one man when she loved two.

Robyn had come from nothing, the very bottom. She'd been dropped off in a church foyer in the dead of night when she was one day old, discarded and unwanted. From that time on, she'd been shipped from foster home to foster home, never belonging, and told she'd never amount to anything. It was easy to believe.

She'd run away from the past and its plethora of dirty memories. Robyn had been determined to reinvent herself, to cast everything about her old life aside. It wasn't easy trying to jump a class, her lowly roots trying to pull her back down.

Now she was falling for a cowboy, reminding her of the painful past she wanted to escape. The city, its fake people, and the never-ending struggle for perfection were the perfect backdrop for a woman broken inside.

"How'd you manage to land two smoking hot cowboys?" asked Shelley when the silence dragged on too long. Reflection was something to be avoided, and everything was coming back now.

"Lucky, I guess." She stared out the window, watching the golden fields pass by. What she should have been doing was ripping Shelly and Peter a new one for abandoning her. She should have been demanding answers, asking where the fuck they'd been for so many days, and not bending over backward.

She'd sold her soul.

There was nothing left. Her adult life and her struggle to become more had been a joke. What good was status and knock-off Prada when she was the same terrified little girl on the inside? She was caught between two worlds, two women, never belonging fully to either.

"I bet you can't wait to get showered and changed," said Peter. "That house, if you can call that hovel a house, looked like it should be quarantined."

She'd normally laugh and agree, but she couldn't. Yukon and Parker were good men, living an honest simple life. When she'd been there, the rest of the world went away, along with the high expectations bearing down on her.

"It was better than sleeping on the streets," she

said, not hiding her resentment.

"We'll go out to dinner tonight. On me." He winked at her, but his looks and swagger no longer affected her. She'd been bitten by another bug. Robyn had two cowboys on her mind. It was just another reason why she couldn't accept Yukon's offer, not when she was just as attracted to his brother. It wouldn't be fair to him. To any of them.

All her ideals were crumbling around her. She wanted to go back to the way things were— uncomplicated. But now that she'd been given a taste of heaven, things may never be the same.

About forty minutes later, they arrived in another small town. This one was much more developed than the last, and the streets were bustling due to the annual rodeo.

"What are we supposed to be doing here?" she asked, looking out the windows at the mix of tourists and locals. White tents were set up in the fields and horse trailers and RVs lined the roads.

"More boundary disputes. Shouldn't take more than a few days," said Peter. "We have a hotel booked. It's not the Hilton, but it's better than what you've had this week."

She didn't bother to speak her mind. Robyn just wanted this assignment to be done and over with. She wondered if she could go back to her regular, comfortable routine when she got back home to her apartment. Or would she forever wonder what could have been?

Chapter Thirteen

By the time he stopped for a break, it was already three o'clock. Yukon had been pushing himself from sunup until sundown for the past three days. He didn't want time to stop and think about Robyn. Only a few days ago, they'd shared the most passionate night of his life. After what she let him do to her body, he was certain she was interested in a relationship. He couldn't have been more wrong.

He'd actually been played by a woman. Now he was starting to understand why Parker had always steered clear of city girls. They were cold and heartless.

Yukon tugged off his t-shirt and wiped the sweat from his forehead. He needed to eat before he worked himself sick. After jumping down from his tractor into the muck, he did a visual sweep of his land. Land that his father had once harvested. He wanted to resent his life, the one that disgusted Robyn, but he couldn't. If he wasn't good enough for her, then it wasn't meant to be.

The screen door slapped shut after he entered the house. Parker was gone, had been since he'd woken up. They hadn't said more than two words since Robyn fucked off. What he wanted to know was where he went all day, every day. He didn't have any job that Yukon knew about, and after hearing about his injuries and doctor visits, he was convinced Parker was riding in the rodeo again.

He made a sandwich and started up the coffee maker. As he glanced out the front bay window, a pick-up truck drove along the long driveway to his house. He took another bite and walked to the side door to see who was coming.

It was Gage's truck.

"Hey, where've you been, stranger?" Gage tossed a cigarette butt as he jumped down from his lifted truck.

"Busy." He went back inside, not sure how he could avoid this conversation. He'd been avoiding all his friends and neighbors since Robyn showed up in town. She'd really done a number on him.

Gage followed him inside.

"Marcy told me about the girl. What happened with that?"

He shook his head. "Long story. One I'm not in the mood for." The carafe was full, so he grabbed a mug from the cupboard and poured a coffee. "Help yourself," he said, leaving the kitchen.

"Since when do you keep details from me?" Gage rooted in the cupboard for a mug. "You've never been shy about kissing and telling before."

"This one was different." He crashed down on the sofa and put his feet up on the coffee table. "Well, fuck, I thought she was."

"You should have known better. I saw the devil in her eyes. You know what they say about city girls."

"Parker likes to remind me plenty," said Yukon.

"What did he have to say about her?"

"I haven't talked with him. He warned me from the start, so I don't want to hear it. We haven't said two words for days."

Gage sat on the arm of the recliner. "Women are overrated. You should be celebrating being a bachelor." He took a sip of coffee. "We've missed you at Meg's. Stop being a stranger."

"I'll be by soon. Just need to get my head on straight." He would. Yukon had to move on and stop moping. His misery wouldn't make anything better. It was time he moved on, and he hoped he could put all memories of Robyn out of his head for good. It was just different now that he was older. He wasn't interested in meaningless hook-ups. What he wanted was something lasting, a relationship with meaning. Maybe the men in his family were cursed to die alone.

Yukon returned to his fields after his break, pouring himself into his work. He had no intention of heading to Meg's yet, not when his head was still a damn mess.

Once the sun had set, the outdoor flood lights illuminating the grounds around the farm, Yukon closed up the barn and made sure everything was secure for the night. He'd sleep good, exhaustion already pulling at him. When he entered the house, Parker was sitting at the dinette table, eating something that smelled like heaven.

Parker must have read his mind, pointing his fork to the oven. "Ms. Granger sent meatloaf."

He helped himself. Ms. Granger was an excellent cook, and Yukon was starved. They sat across from each other at the tiny table, eating and not speaking. Only the clink of cutlery against china could be heard.

"You've been quiet," said Parker.

"There's a lot of work to be done around the house." He implied that Parker wouldn't know since he was always gone all day.

"I'm sure there is," said Parker. "Was there any more damage from the storm?"

He narrowed his eyes. "This is *our* ranch, so why am I the only one working the land?"

"Farming doesn't put food on the table these days, does it? I have some side jobs. Don't worry about it." Parker continued to eat.

Yukon put his fork down, leaning back in his chair. "Stop bullshitting me. You're bull riding again, aren't you?"

"Fuck no."

"That why've you been to the doctor at least twice this month? What kind of side job gets your ribs kicked in?"

"Drop it," Parker warned. "You're not my mother, so stop acting like it."

"Well, I thought you knew what it meant to keep your word. Most cowboys in this town have the kind of honor you can take to the bank."

Parker bolted to his feet, his chair scraping along the tiles. He pointed his finger accusatorily in Yukon's face. "You best watch your mouth." Then he tossed his napkin on the table and left the room. Yukon could hear him taking the stairs to the second level.

Why was he lying? What was he hiding? He should have the balls to admit he was in the rodeo again.

Yukon hoped to open a dialog, to get some fucking answers, but he didn't want to push it any further. He was dead tired, and his spirits were still in the dumps after Robyn stomped on his heartstrings. It would take time for him to feel like himself, but then again, that would only mean wanting more.

He walked to the front windows and looked out at the moon. Was it mocking him? Was God out there listening? Yukon had never felt so alone in his life. He'd been taught to man the fuck up from an early age, and staying strong was the only thing keeping him going. To what end? He was middle-aged, lonely, and craved a woman … no, one woman. Why was happiness always dangling just out of reach?

Yukon felt like he was being punished, destined to suffer to the end like his father. His old man wasn't a saint, but he'd loved their mother something fierce. Yukon wanted to feel that passion, to work for more than dollars and cents. He wanted to provide for a woman, for a family of his own. When he envisioned that perfect scenario, Parker always came to mind. As much as they bickered and fought, they only had each other. They'd taken care of one another most of their lives, so the thought of moving on without Parker sent an uneasy feeling to his gut.

There were no easy answers.

****

Parker paced his room, feeling like a caged animal. Everything was coming unraveled, and he blamed it all on Robyn and her fickle nature. There'd been one time he'd fallen in love. Or so he'd believed at the time. It was almost two decades ago when that city girl had taken him for a ride. He'd been traveling the rodeo circuit and the girl with her book smarts and blonde curls lured him in, only to use and discard him like worthless country trash when she was through. She laughed when she told her friends about their time together. It had all been a joke to her, a fling with the brainless bronc rider. Ever since that day, he kept his distance from stuck-up bitches who thought they were better than him.

Robyn should have been different, but apparently he was still a bad judge of character when it came to women. It didn't matter. He couldn't give a shit one way or another now that Robyn had rushed off without a backward glance. It was Yukon he worried about. His brother had been pushing himself harder, pulling away from friends, and he looked like shit.

He should have a heart-to-heart with Yukon, but he wasn't up to it. That siren had worked her wiles on him, too. He could still remember the scent of her perfume and the curve of her ass. Her crocodile tears were just that, and he wouldn't be a victim. He'd never hand over his heart to a woman again, certainly not a city girl.

Parker looked at himself in the mirror, twisting at an angle to get a good look at the healing bruises on his side, now a faint purple. He should have known better, but at least he was on the mend.

He had another early start in the morning, so he needed to clear his head and get some damn rest. His dream was to work his own land with Yukon, make enough to live comfortably. With all their bad luck lately, it would be a while before that day came.

Parker lifted the crystal top off the decanter he kept on his dresser and poured himself a drink. He downed it in one swallow, feeling the burn all the way down his throat to his stomach. He poured another.

Robyn was probably laughing about them right now. Her and her asshole boyfriend.

After another hit of hard liquor, he hoped sleep would come quickly.

****

The next morning, his alarm woke him from a dead sleep. He sat up and scrubbed his hands over his face, feeling worse than shit after overindulging. After a quick shower to wake himself up, he made himself some oatmeal in the kitchen. He could hear Yukon milling around upstairs, and truthfully he wanted to be gone before he came downstairs. Any conversation with his brother would lead to more lies, and he was tired of the lies and games.

He shoveled the hot oatmeal into his mouth as he stood by the front window. The sun was just starting to lighten the sky, hints of deep pinks and reds peeking from behind the treeline. A rooster from the next farm over crowed.

"Another early start?"

Fuck.

He didn't turn around. Or answer.

Yukon stood beside him, taking in the same view. He took a sip of his juice.

"Seems we're becoming strangers, you and I. That the way you want it?" asked Yukon.

"Things are fucked up lately."

"You don't have to do whatever it is you're doing. We can get twice as much done on the farm if you help out."

"It still won't be enough. Times are tough for crop farmers."

Yukon finished his juice. "At what point are you going to give things a chance? We're supposed to be a team."

He knew his brother was talking about his promise never to ride in the rodeos again. Yukon expected him to listen, but he refused to do the same. The real issue with Yukon was that woman. He'd been moping ever since Robyn left.

"Don't be a hypocrite, Yukon. You're pissed I don't listen to you, but wasn't I the one to tell you to stay away from Robyn?"

"I really don't want to hear her name."

Parker scoffed. "At least you got something out of it."

Yukon whirled on him, shoving him backward. "I didn't want her for sex. I wanted to fucking keep her. Some of us think with more than our dicks."

"And I warned you she'd break your fucking heart, didn't I?" Parker wasn't about to tell his brother the pathetic tale of his own broken heart so many years ago. He was protecting Yukon from the same heartache. City girls were good for nothing.

"Don't worry about me. Do I look like a boy? I'm past having my heart broken."

"Tell that to someone who'll believe your

bullshit," said Parker.

Yukon's body looked tense, his muscles rigid. He probably wanted to brawl and let off steam, but he held back, finally raising his arms to the side in defeat. "What do you want from me, Parker? You want us to live alone in this damn house forever? You want us to die like Dad?"

Parker was at a loss for words. He may come across as an asshole, but he wanted Yukon happy. He'd sacrifice anything for his younger brother because his love life was already a forfeit. That was how family worked. With his heart stomped on, Yukon could only see his pain, and refused to see that Parker had been trying to warn him the entire time.

He shook his head.

"Tell me the truth about one thing, Parker. I saw the way you looked at her. Tell me you didn't love her."

His first reaction was to lie. He was good at that lately. But Yukon asked for the truth. He wasn't sure what the truth was, only that there had been something there—a connection, lust, desire, he wasn't sure what the fuck it was. "Yeah, I felt something, but does it even matter? She's gone, which means she's no good for either of us."

Yukon took a deep breath, running both hands through his hair.

"Don't think about her. You know the best way to do that? Get out there and stop spending all your free time daydreaming," said Parker.

Yukon nodded and returned to the kitchen, setting his glass in the sink. "I'll see you later." The screen door flapped shut a minute later.

He should take his own advice, but he'd been using cheap whiskey to stave off the loneliness and disappointment. Every time he remembered the day he caught Robyn rooting around his room, he'd get an instant hard-on. As much as he knew she was a mistake, he still wanted her. She was a forbidden temptation, and those were the hardest to forget.

Chapter Fourteen

Robyn had spent the last few days going over paperwork with different farmers and representatives. Now that it was Monday, they had to close the Palmer account. One of their smaller properties was on affected land, so they had to get them to sign off for the lowest price possible. Since Shelly had other clients to deal with in the morning, aka mani and pedi, Peter was doing the driving.

"Robyn?"

"Sorry, did you say something?" asked Robyn. Her head had been in the clouds lately. She kept trying to shut out her memories of Yukon and Parker, but they kept forcing their way back to the surface. She wasn't the type to fuck a man and run, and it was usually the other way around. It was the fact the brothers brought her past to the forefront, made her feel things she'd been trying to bottle up all her life. They were her kryptonite.

She kept telling herself to move forward, keep her head up, and reach for the end goal. Cowboys may not have the same aspirations. Apparently they cared about family, not money and success. Robyn didn't do family, so she needed to keep climbing the corporate ladder one rung at a time.

"I was talking about the Palmer account," he said. "We need to get this signed at the lowest possible price, so put on the charm. These bushmen can probably be swayed easily, if you know what I mean."

"Yeah, I got you."

She looked out the window and rolled her eyes. He wanted her to pop open a few buttons and flirt her way into a favorable contract. Some days she felt the only reason she got anywhere in court was by using her sexuality. Then Shelly would remind her that was their super power.

Robyn exhaled, trying not to get so damn psychological. What she needed was the city, the lights, the noise, the late nights at Metrosexual.

These strange beds and the rural countryside were stripping her defenses back layer by layer, making her weaker. Her real parents, whoever the fuck they were, were simpletons from a small country town. She wanted to be nothing like them. She needed to be so much more.

"We're here," said Peter.

Again, she'd been deep in her own dire thoughts. She grabbed her briefcase and exited the vehicle, straightening her skirt suit after taking a couple steps. This ranch was different from the others they'd visited last week. It was a large, modern operation with a huge workforce.

"This is what I'm talking about. If I had to rough it in the country, I'd like to stay with these guys." Peter pointed to the house in the distance. It was a ranch-style home, but looked like it cost a small fortune. This Palmer family owned a shitload of property and ran the largest cattle operation in the province. She hoped they didn't have their own high-priced lawyers ready to push for top dollar.

"I just want to get home. Like yesterday." She watched each step, her heels sinking into the muck.

The sounds of cowboys hollering, cattle clamouring, and horns blaring were an audible overload. A feed truck started backing up right in front of her, putting her on her last nerve. She barely darted out of the path of the splattering mud. Shelly owed her for ditching this signing. Her friend wanted to look good for dinner tonight. She planned to get Peter in her bed, which would leave Robyn stuck in limbo since they were sharing a room. Three was definitely a crowd in this case.

Her train of thought led her back to that old house. She envisioned a threesome with Yukon and Parker and was shocked by the strong urge that raced through her body. Stupid hormones. Her body was still thrumming from that one night with Yukon. The man did his boot size justice, but there was no way she was going to tell Shelly her theory was right. If she let her friend know she'd fucked a hillbilly, she'd never let her live it down. In their world, the higher the degree or paycheck, the stronger the bragging rights.

There had been times she wanted more, wanted real love, but reality was usually quick to douse those flames. One lesson had aided her well. The harder the veneer, the easier it was to get through life.

"There's the office entrance," said Peter.

They entered the one-story brick building. The waiting area was dated but better than what she'd seen the last few days. The secretary looked way too young.

"We're here to see Mr. Palmer," said Peter.

The girl smiled. "Which one?"

Robyn frowned and pulled out a file, sifting through the pages. "Austin?"

"Sure. Just a minute."

"Is Austin the father?" asked Peter.

"No idea. It's on one of the papers."

A minute later, a tall, buffed man came out from the back, the girl following behind him.

"Morning. I'm Austin Palmer." He held his hand out to Peter, then shook Robyn's. The man wasn't the father of this cattle enterprise. He only looked to be in his mid-forties with dirty-blond hair and striking blue eyes. She immediately thought of Yukon and cursed herself.

"Is there somewhere we can get these files signed off on?" asked Peter. "We're a long way from home."

The cowboy waved them to follow.

"How many Mr. Palmers work here? Your secretary wasn't sure which one we wanted to see," asked Peter.

"Oh, that's our baby sister, Amy. And there are three of us now, me and my two younger brothers. Our father passed away not too long ago."

"I'm sorry to hear that."

"Come on in." Austin held open a door down the hall and waited for them to enter. It was a conference-style room, exactly what Robyn was used to. She put her briefcase down and set the files on the table with two pens at the side. Then she remembered what Peter had said in the car, so she hooked her suit jacket on the back on the chair. Robyn didn't have to do much to make herself more noticeable. Her curves were usually a hindrance. At work, they often got her points.

As Peter and Austin made small talk, she glanced out the large picture window that looked out onto the grounds. Farm hands were leading horses, driving tractors with bales of hay, and doing various odd jobs. It was quite the commotion. Then she caught sight of something familiar, making her sit straighter in her seat. She looked closer, hoping the cowboy would turn around so she could get a better look.

He entered one of the barns.

Robyn turned around and focused on the task at hand.

"I like having friends," said Austin. "In my line of work, I find good friends are more valuable than a few dollars."

"You're absolutely right, Mr. Palmer."

"Of course, my father also taught us to keep our enemies even closer." He winked at them, taking special interest in Robyn. This man may be a cowboy, but at least he had money and class. Still, she couldn't garner up enough interest to give a shit. Her heart was still warring with her, but she'd win the battle soon enough.

The papers were finally signed, and they packed up and said their usual pleasantries. She was tiring of this traveling legal freak show and wanted to go home. *Out of sight, out of mind*, or so she hoped.

"Take a look around, enjoy the views before you head out," said Austin. "As I tell all my guests, our home is your home."

"You're too kind, Mr. Palmer. I hope to have the pleasure of doing business with you again," said Peter. If he was Calloway's right-hand man, he was a professional ass-kisser. It was part of the business.

They walked back toward their rental car. She kept an eye on the barn she'd seen through the window. Then she saw him.

Parker.

He turned around after setting down a wheelbarrow, and they made eye contract. Fuck, he looked sexier than sin. His plaid shirt was unbuttoned, his chest tanned and slick with sweat. He ran a hand through his dark hair, his eyes narrowed with too much hate for her to handle.

She rushed alongside Peter, wanting to be anywhere else. Why was Parker at the Palmer ranch anyway? She thought she'd never see the brothers again. This was not part of her plan.

When they reached the car, it was blocked in by a pick-up truck to the front and a massive pile of cow shit to the rear.

"Double parked in a field. That's luck for you," said Peter. "Can you get one of these hired hands to move this thing?"

She set her briefcase on the hood of the car and

traipsed back toward the house. *What a gentleman.* Her shoes were not made for this environment. The muck even reached the top of her foot, the cool mud leaking into her shoe. She bent down to inspect the damage.

"Thought you'd be back in the city by now."

Robyn looked up into those familiar dark eyes. "I'm heading home soon. I said I still had business to finish."

"Guess you did." He licked his dry lips, looking down at her with no emotion on his face.

"I didn't know you worked here," she said, looking around the vast property. Why would he work here rather than on his family ranch?

"Bills need to be paid."

Peter came out to meet them. "What's going on? Do you have the keys for that pick-up truck?" he asked. She noticed the moment Peter recognized Parker, and she didn't like the smug look on his face.

"You have business here, too?" asked Peter. "Is your brother with you?"

He shook his head.

"You're quiet now. Let me guess, you work for Mr. Palmer?" Peter chuckled, and Robyn cringed. She'd usually laugh along with him, now it all felt wrong. "If he doesn't keep up with minimum wage, you let me know. I'll have my legal team look into it."

"We should ask for the keys in the office," said Robyn.

"Right. You wouldn't have the keys to the trucks, would you? You're just hired to haul the horse shit, eh, boy?" Peter checked his Rolex. "Robyn, could you get someone with the keys? I need to wait in the car. The smell is getting to me."

Parker hadn't moved. Hadn't said a word.

She expected his type to knock Peter a new one.

The cowboy was twice the size and made of raw, chiseled muscle. Of course, she'd noticed then and now. She suddenly realized she was more attracted to this working man than the guy earning six figures. It was so out of character for her.

"Sorry about that," she said.

"Don't lose any sleep over it, sweetheart," he said. "I wouldn't expect any different. You're all the same."

Her mouth fell agape, but then again, she'd just fucked over him and his brother. Parker had told her to stay away and she hadn't listened. It wasn't like she forced herself on Yukon.

"You don't know me," she said.

"I've seen more than enough." He started to walk away.

"Hey, I didn't see Yukon complaining."

Parker did a half turn. "That's because he believed you were a good girl."

She wanted to shout that she *was* a good girl, but who was she kidding. Robyn was a mess on the inside, even if she managed to hold her exterior together. Her façade was fracturing like aging china. Of everyone, it was Parker who saw through her bullshit, down to the marrow.

It seemed like a lifetime before they were back on the road heading to their hotel. The surprise visit with Parker had rattled her. She never expected to see him again, and now had to start forgetting all over again. It wasn't easy when he looked so damn good. Even worse was the way he made her feel. She wasn't a bad person—just messed up, trying to make it in the world like everyone else. Robyn didn't want him to think she was a bitch.

****

Parker set his empty beer bottle on the counter. Marcy walked up to him, resting her hip against the counter. "Problems, honey?"

"You have no idea, darlin'. For my troubles, a beer just won't cut it."

Marcy grabbed a shot glass from under the counter.

"Just one?"

She smirked and grabbed another. "Sounds like woman troubles to me."

He shook his head. "There's no woman."

"Maybe that's the problem." She finished pouring the amber liquid into his waiting glasses.

Usually, some of his friends were at Meg's at this time of night, but for once he was glad for the alone time. Parker just wanted to drown some of his sorrows in more booze. It was a Band-Aid fix, but it was all he had at his disposal. Seeing Robyn in the flesh again, looking so fucking hot in her tight little suit, brought back all his feelings—hate, anger, lust, and betrayal.

Even worse was being mocked by that little prick in front of her. If Parker had acted on his desire to pound him into the earth, he would have lost his job. He was lucky to get it in the first place, and he didn't have the luxury to risk it. So, he had to suck it up and take everything the rich suit dished out. Robyn was no different. She'd royally screwed over his brother.

"What are you drinking?"

Speak of the devil. He'd recognize that voice anywhere. In fact, it was haunting his dreams. "Whiskey."

"A little early for that, isn't it?"

Parker looked at his watch. It was 6:30. He'd just gotten off work a while earlier and came straight to Meg's Longhorn. "Whatever." Then he turned to look at

Robyn as she struggled up onto the stool next to him. "Why are you here?"

"I was hoping to run into you."

He scoffed, swallowing the first shot. "Why's that?"

"Look, I didn't mean to hurt your brother. I swear."

"Yukon fucks a different woman every night. You were the flavor of the week, and he sure as hell moved on in a hurry," he lied. "Why don't you run home to pretty boy? Country living will eat you alive."

She stayed silent for the longest time. Long enough for him to feel a tinge of guilt.

"I just thought… Never mind. Forget I came here."

Parker slipped off his stool, downed the next shot, and then grabbed Robyn by the upper arm. He brought her to the small hallway near the bathrooms where they could be alone.

"What do you think you're doing?"

"Listen, little lady. I don't know why the fuck you came here. First you tell me you're sorry about screwing over Yukon, then when you think he's moved on, your feelings are hurt. Which is it?" he asked. "You can't have it both ways. You want him or you don't."

He had her pinned between the wall and his body.

"I don't know why I came."

"You said you came looking for me," he said. "Well, I'm right here."

They stared at each other, the heat between them palpable. Why was he so damn attracted to her? Women had always been disposable to him, but Robyn was impossible to let go.

"I—"

Before she could continue, he cupped her face

and kissed her on the mouth. Rather than pull away, she melted against his body, kissing him with a desperate hunger. Her lips were soft, and she tasted all woman. He closed his eyes, kissing her with the intensity of the pent-up emotions he'd been harboring.

She slipped her hands under his t-shirt and slid them up his back. Feeling her skin to skin made his cock harder than oak. He wanted to hoist her up against the wall and fuck her, sink deep into her heat. Instead, he broke their kiss. He braced one hand on the wall near her head, and the other had a mind of its own. Parker ran the backs of his fingers down her side, over the swell of her breast until he reached her waist. He reached back and cupped her ass, tugging her against the hardness of his body.

"That what you want?" he asked.

Her lips were swollen, her lipstick askew. The poor thing could barely catch her breath, her chest rising and falling in deep waves. "You're an asshole."

He smirked. "And you still want me to fuck you, don't you?"

Robyn scowled, her brows furrowed as she tried to wrestle him away.

"Relax, baby girl. Just teasing." He tilted her chin up and leaned down to kiss her neck. Parker teased her pulse point, then whispered in her ear. "You're so fucking beautiful."

Chapter Fifteen

Robyn was a basket case. Why did Parker have such a profound effect on her? The moment he kissed her, she went spineless, every cell in her body under his control. He was so strong, so purely masculine that she was putty in his hands. His kiss was passion untamed, his rough stubble scraping her cheeks.

When he grabbed her ass, pulling her close, she felt his erection. The man was just as impressive as his brother. The volatile mix of hate and desire she felt for Parker was at a boiling point.

"Don't compliment me. We both know how you really feel," she said.

She knew he barely tolerated her during her stay at his house. His hatred for city people was impossible to mask. Robyn represented everything he hated, so she wasn't going to fall for his tricks again.

"I know how I feel. What about you, baby? You ready to choose a cowboy who shovels horse shit over your high-priced lawyer?" He chuckled. "Don't try and tell me I judge you because you're no different. You think you're too good for us, that's why you're running away."

She wanted to protest, to tell him he was full of shit, but he was right. As usual. She was judging them on their bank accounts, occupation, and education. It was what she'd always done, what all the women she associated with did. Then again, Shelly and the other Barbie dolls in the city didn't believe love existed, while Robyn still desperately hoped it was real.

She struggled financially, not ready to sell her body for the right account. It was a full-time job trying to keep up appearances, but she kept doing it, kept trying to be accepted.

Parker saw through everything.

"I don't belong here," she whispered. Where did she belong? She felt like a leaf on the wind, trying to hide from the past and sabotaging her own happiness at every turn.

"You have a man waiting for you in the city? Or is it the asshole from earlier?"

"I don't have a man. If I did, I wouldn't have slept with Yukon," she said.

He narrowed his eyes. "Do you make a habit of fucking strange men while away on business?"

She shoved him in the chest, but the brick house didn't budge. "Fuck you."

"Tell me something real, Robyn. What are you hiding?"

"I'm not hiding anything. I have a great life. I couldn't be happier." She felt the burn of unshed tears building up. Her apartment in the city sucked, and the only reason she went out with friends was to avoid focusing on how miserable and lonely she was. Her past kept nipping at her heels, forcing her to up her game to avoid it.

"Yukon may believe all your bullshit, but you can't fool me."

"What do you want to hear? That I'm nowhere I hoped to be at my age, that I'm treading water most days, that the older I get the more contracts I lose?" She couldn't believe she was unloading so much personal baggage to this virtual stranger. "Would that make you happier?"

He smiled. "Was that so hard?" Parker took her hand and led her through the diner. "Marcy, put the drinks on my tab, darlin'," he shouted to the waitress.

Once outside, he pointed to his truck. The old,

navy pick-up with patches of rust screamed masculinity. She'd always convinced herself that a Mercedes or BMW was the measure of a man—God was she ever wrong.

Once in the passenger side, he started up the ignition and drove off.

"Where we going?" she asked.

"Somewhere more private. I want to talk."

She was done talking. Robyn had already said too much, breaking all her rules. But she didn't want to be alone, didn't want to make the long drive back to her hotel. She craved to be near Parker, wanted to see how far he'd push her. If she were honest with herself, she missed the brothers, missed their simple lives together— even if only for a few days.

He didn't drive too far away, pulling along a winding dirt driveway in the middle of nowhere. They stopped when they reached an old barn. It must have been an impressive red in its heyday, but now it was weather worn, only a faint reminder of the original color.

Parker got out of the truck. "Come on," he said before shutting the door behind him.

Robyn stepped out, less than gracefully. She really should have changed clothes, but as soon as she'd gotten back to the hotel with Peter, she took the car and went looking for Parker.

"Where are we?" she asked, walking through the tall, unkempt grass. The sun was already setting, the distant forest blurred out into shadows, notes of orange and pink highlighting the clouds. She took a deep breath, savoring the scent of the fields after the rain.

"A secret place."

He slid open one of the side bay doors, the rusty old rollers breaking the hush of twilight. Hay dust rained down before they entered. She followed behind him as he began to climb up a rickety ladder in the center of the barn. With her high heels and tight skirt, it was a major effort. At least there was no one coming up after her as her skirt was creased at her upper thighs.

When she made it to the top, there was no sign of Parker. She struggled to get to her feet and adjust her clothes. Robyn stepped out of her heels and shrugged out of her jacket, hanging it on a hook. She found Parker standing precariously close to the edge of an open hayloft. The view was breathtaking, rolling hills that seemed to go on forever. Mixed with the morphing sky, it was better than any painting.

"That's quite a view," she said. Robyn stood to the side, so she could have part of her body safely behind the wooden planks. It was a long drop down.

"I like to come here when I need to think. In a couple hours, there'll be more stars than you've ever seen." He had his arms folded over his chest. When he turned his head to the side, his eyes were hypnotic. "Come here."

She shook her head. "I'm scared of heights."

"Promise I won't let you fall."

Robyn cautiously stepped toward Parker. He was a lot taller than her, his frame twice her size. He took her hand and brought her down to sit with him, their legs dangling over the edge.

"Why are we really here, Parker?"

He chuckled, a deep masculine sound. "I don't even know," he said. "I keep telling myself not to waste my time on you. To forget you ever showed up on our doorstep." He leaned over his knees, looking out onto the darkening horizon. "You must have touched a nerve."

"I thought you were worried about Yukon."

"I always worry about him. You don't think it's possible for two men to love the same woman?"

She shrugged. "Love's a big word."

"Have you ever been in love?"

Robyn didn't even know what the fuck love was. She'd never been loved and wasn't even sure what it would look like if she found it. Her friends thought she was crazy for believing in the concept of true love, Shelly even saying she had fairy tale sickness.

The closest she'd come was last week at their house. She'd never felt so carefree and wanted in her life. Maybe she had fallen in love—to two cowboy brothers.

"No, but I'm not even sure there's such a thing. Maybe it was created by Hallmark or something."

"There're different kinds of love, I suppose. I mean, I loved my parents, I love Yukon, I love my truck." He chuckled. "But when it comes to women, I kind of gave up on that kind of love years ago."

"Why?"

"I'm forty-five, darlin'. That's no spring chicken. I think the time for love passed me by when I wasn't looking."

That made her sad. He reminded her so much of herself. Robyn also felt like she'd missed the bus.

****

Parker should have been home, getting some sleep, not in their old barn with Robyn. He'd told Yukon to forget about her and move on, but here he was, falling for the city girl. There was a sweetness about her, something that made her different. She wasn't who she said she was, but a woman playing a role not meant for her.

"You don't look too old," she whispered.

He looked deep into her eyes. "Who'd fall for a washed-up cowboy like me?"

"Any woman with eyes."

Parker smiled. "So you like what you see?"

"You're not too bad for a country boy."

He felt comfortable with Robyn, a unique connection between them. "What about you? Why no husband?"

"I don't know."

"Too busy with work?" he asked. "One day you'll wake up alone and bitter like me. Don't make the same mistake."

"In my circles, women have to be perfect. I'm getting too old to compete in business, never mind finding a man."

"Where you're from sounds like a crazy place. It's simpler here. Right here, right now, you're more than perfect." He leaned in, using a hand to bring her face closer. Parker brushed his lips over hers, then kissed her softly, tentatively. This was nothing like the volatile passion at the diner, this felt real—to him anyway.

He expected he'd have his heart broken by Robyn again, but if Yukon could man up and handle it, so could he. Some sins were worth the price.

"I'll be heading home tomorrow," she said.

He ignored her, stealing any more words away with his kisses. Parker tugged off his shirt and laid in on the hay behind her. He got to his hands and knees, bringing her away from the edge and under him. "You're invading my dreams, baby girl. All I can think about is fucking you."

Parker started unbuttoning her fancy blouse, but lost patience and tugged it open with both hands. Her white lace bra barely contained her big tits, and they jiggled for a few moments.

He leaned down and trailed kissed down her neck to the swell of her breast. She ran her hands over his bare shoulders, her fingers combing into the hair at the nape of his neck. "Parker…"

"Tell me you want me to fuck you, baby." He kept moving down her body, fiddling with the zipper on her skirt and pulling it all the way off.

"We shouldn't do this," she said.

He spread her legs apart, the darkness of her pussy visible through the white panties. Parker ran a finger along her inner thigh until he reached the elastic edge. He slipped two fingers under the fabric, brushing them over her clit. She gasped and bucked, her body a live wire.

"You have no idea how good I can make you feel. Just relax. Forget tomorrow. Today it's just us."

She didn't retort, her lips parted as she fought for breath. He sat up on his knees, staring down at her in just her bra and panties, her legs bent and splayed for him.

He hooked his fingers at the waistband of her underpants and tugged them off, opening her legs again once she was bare. She fought him, trying to keep her knees shut.

"Don't hide that pretty pussy from me, sweetheart. Let me enjoy myself. You're my little piece of heaven right now."

Parker kissed the inside of her knee. He kept his eyes on hers as he worked his way closer to her cunt. He wanted to eat her until she screamed his name. No one would hear her way out here. He'd show her that, unlike city boys, country boys liked to get dirty.

This had been their first barn before the new one was built near the house, and they hadn't used it for storage in decades. It was still his personal escape from time to time. As a boy, he played here with Yukon, shooting their rifles, drinking their dad's moonshine, or talking about girls. That was a long time ago.

There was minimal lighting inside the barn now, but enough for him to see her pink folds. His cock strained in his jeans just looking at her gorgeous body. How could any man refuse a woman like Robyn?

He dropped down on his elbows, swiping his tongue up her slick folds. She cried out.

"Parker!" She reached for his head. "What are you doing?"

"Showing you how a man should worship a woman's body." He squeezed her thick thighs with his hands, getting comfortable before suckling her clit into his mouth. She squirmed beneath him, grabbing at the hay to her sides. He didn't give her any reprieve, fucking her with this tongue, licking and sucking her sensitive little bud. Parker could live between her legs.

It didn't take long for her to relax, her nervous energy fading away as a new wanton desire took over her body. Her legs dropped heavily to the sides, her breathing slow and shallow.

"Oh God, Parker. That feels so good." Her feminine moans drove him crazy.

He almost let her come. It would only take him a few moments to bring her to a screaming finale, but he wanted to be deep inside her, to feel her milking his cock when it happened.

Parker began to kiss higher, up her stomach toward those beautiful tits. He reached behind her and unlatched her bra, her breasts slipping to the sides when he tossed it.

"So damn beautiful," he muttered as he cupped her tits, bringing them together. "Big and juicy." He began to engorge himself on her mountainous cleavage, flicking her nipples with his tongue until she was panting harder.

"Please, Parker."

"What do you want, baby?"

"I need you."

Parker braced himself over her body, leaning in to kiss her once on the mouth. "What do you need, Robyn?"

"You. Your cock."

He smirked. "I like the sound of you talking dirty. Turns me on." Parker unbuckled and then unzipped his jeans. He released his erection, hard and heavy. "This what you want?"

She nodded, her lips parted.

After kicking off his jeans, he dropped down, kissing her neck and nipping her ear. She wrapped her arms around his shoulders.

"Make love to me."

Chapter Sixteen

What was she saying? This was just sex, sating that burning lust between them. Or was it?

Robyn had been in an internal conflict since arriving in the small town. The cowboy brothers snared her, tilting her entire world off its axis. Should she keep resisting, fighting for her pointless ideals? Or should she take a risk and reach for that fairy tale?

"Yes, ma'am."

Parker's muscles flexed as he supported his weight over her body. He'd already proved he was a godsend in bed, his wicked tongue bringing her higher than she'd ever been. Men usually shied away from dirty sex, making her feel embarrassed or uncomfortable if she suggested anything out of the ordinary. Not Parker. He made her feel like a goddess, all her locked-up sexuality allowed to break free.

He ran the head of his cock over her pussy, teasing over and over until she was arching up in a poor attempt to capture his length. He'd left her dangling on the edge, desperate for more. He knew exactly what he was doing, and his experience only turned her on more.

"I need you, Parker."

She did. Not just sex, but love … forever. For once in her entire life, she wanted to let go and allow someone else to take the reins. She remembered his tattoo. Robyn needed to have courage, despite her fears, and take what she wanted. She wanted Yukon and Parker. Could they love her together? Could she say goodbye to everything she'd ever known and trust them not to abandon her?

"I need you too, baby." He filled her with his big cock. She gasped, savoring the fullness. Loving the connection of having Parker inside her. She had the urge to tell him she loved him, to beg him not to break her heart, but she kept silent. "You feel better than I imagined. You're squeezing my cock like a fist."

"You're so big."

"It's all yours, if you want it," he said. Parker began to fuck her, pumping his lean hips like a piston. She could see the stars start to appear from the open hayloft. Robyn held him tighter, never wanting to let go. All the memories of their days together came back, and she was transported to those happy moments. The happiest of her pathetic life.

"Yes," she murmured. The thought of Parker making love to another woman was indigestible. She wanted him for herself. Wanted his brother just as much.

He worked her body, slamming into her over and over. The man was skilled, every thrust of his hips bringing her closer. They kissed and held each other, the warm breeze caressing the clean sweat on their nude bodies. When her orgasm started to spark, she dug her nails into his back.

"That's a girl," he said. "Come for me, baby. I want to fill you up and make you mine."

Yes, she wanted to be his. His woman. His everything.

Her womb began to contract, and she panted as her orgasm reached its peak. She exploded, screaming Parker's name, her contractions squeezing his cock until she felt him come. He growled, his muscles going taut as he filled her with his cum.

Parker exhaled, rolling to his back. She looked at his body, completely naked, partially concealed by shadows. Even flaccid, his cock was impressive. "Thank you," he said.

She crawled over to him, his cum leaking down

her inner thigh. "Tell me you love me," she said.

He narrowed his eyes, looking at her with a mix of confusion.

"Please."

He twisted to his side, running his hand into her hair and securing her head in one place. "Say that again."

"Tell me you love me."

"Don't play with me, Robyn."

"I'm not."

He tugged her head back and she let out a little gasp of pain. Parker licked along her jaw before nipping her ear. He kissed her on the mouth, deep and possessive. "I could stay here forever. With you. But—"

She shook her head, not wanting to hear it.

"I can't fuck Yukon over. If you have to choose, choose him."

Her eyes filled with tears. She felt so vulnerable, so completely exposed. "Why can't I have you both?" She bit the inside of her lip after daring to spit out the most important, raw question plaguing her thoughts. It could cost her both men. But she couldn't bury the truth forever.

The way they'd toyed with her in their horse barn and by the fireplace. It had felt natural for them to share her, but maybe it was all in her head. They were brothers, after all. This could be a deal breaker.

He shut her up with another kiss, his tongue caressing hers. Robyn never did get what she asked for.

****

The next morning, Parker needed a cold shower to wake up. He could barely keep his eyes open. He'd been up until late with Robyn before driving her back to the diner so she could get her car. Watching her leave had been one of the hardest things he'd ever done. It wasn't easy keeping up a stone-cold exterior, but he wouldn't let her break his heart. She'd already done a good job of that with his brother.

She was heading back to the city today, just as he predicted she would. His brother foolishly believed she'd give up her fancy lifestyle for him, but Parker knew better. They had nothing worthwhile to offer a woman like Robyn.

He was out in the barn saddling his horse when Yukon came in. His shadow blocked out the early morning rays.

"No work today?" asked Yukon.

"Not today."

"What're you doing with Silver?"

"I'm taking a ride. Do I have your permission?" He backed out his gelding, forcing Yukon to move out of the way. He wasn't in the mood for the third degree. As much as he hated to admit it to himself, Robyn took a piece of him when she left. Making love to her under the stars had meant something. But it wasn't meant to last.

"You getting practice in for the barrel racing?" asked Yukon.

He growled as he led Silver to the paddock. His horse had been his sidekick when he was in his rodeo heyday, but he'd been retired ever since Parker stopped competing. "Stop worrying about me and worry about your damn self."

"I don't know what's happened to you. You used to give a shit. Now all you do is sneak around and get drunk. Is that how you want to live your life?"

"Fuck off, Yukon. You're the one pining over a piece of pussy."

Yukon gave him a shove, and Parker laughed. Within seconds they were brawling in the dirt, throwing punching and roughhousing like they did when they were teens. They were matched size for size, but Parker needed the physical outlet as much as Yukon.

After a hard right hook to his jaw, his brother paused, then dropped his fist. "Whatever. You do your thing, I'll do mine." Yukon walked off back to the house.

Parker rubbed his face and cracked his neck to the side. He mounted Silver and tore out into the fields. How much was one man expected to take? He'd been trying to be the head of the house, take care of Yukon, and keep food on the table. Life wasn't easy for them, but he fucking tried every single day.

Now they were in their forties, both single, both growing bitterer by the day. Yukon was right—they were heading down the same path as their father, and there was nothing either of them could do about it. Parker wished Yukon could have found that happily ever after with Robyn. He still remembered the goofy look on his face when he came home from Meg's that first day. It had been the look of a boy in love, and it suited him.

He brought his horse into a full gallop, savoring the feel of the wind on his face. Why couldn't he get Robyn off his mind? He should have fought for her, told her she belonged to them.

Them?

She'd actually said she wanted both of them. Was it even possible to love two men? Was she screwing with him? He didn't take her for the kind of woman to sleep around, but she'd fucked both of them in the same week. The thought of sharing her with Yukon didn't even bother him, which was scarier than anything. If he even mentioned the idea of his lovesick brother, he'd probably knock him into next week.

It didn't matter. She was gone. Back to the city. Back to her real life.

He needed to talk, but not with Yukon. Parker rode his horse through the back paths to Carlson's ranch.

He dismounted when he reached the fence line of their property and walked Silver the rest of the way.

Ava was climbing down from the roof of the house.

"What the heck are you doing up there?"

She stepped off the final rung of the metal ladder. "Fixing the shingles. We had some leaks during the rain storm," she said.

"Carlson around?"

Ava shrugged, adjusting the hammer in her tool belt. "He was helping Wade fix his truck earlier. Check by the barn."

Parker continued to walk his horse toward their barn. They'd grown up with the three Wright kids. Carlson and his identical twin Wade and their younger sister Ava. Nobody messed with her, not just because she had two brothers, but she was more of a cowboy than all of them put together. They didn't have a mother, so he guessed she just never learned how to be a woman.

He spotted Carlson, and he tied Silver to one of the tie outs.

"Hey, stranger," said Carlson. "Where've you been hiding?"

"Working my ass off."

Carlson took off his hat and brushed the dust off his jeans. "Yukon was complaining you're never home."

"I got a side job." Parker didn't want to tell anyone, but he trusted Carlson to keep his mouth shut. "With the Palmers."

Carlson laughed out loud. Parker gave him a shove.

"I'm serious."

"No, you're not."

He ran a hand through his hair, trying to focus on the reason he was there in the first place. "Don't tell

Yukon. Don't tell anyone. Sometimes you have to do shit you don't want to do."

"Okay. I get it."

Carlson knew how much Parker and Yukon hated the Palmer brothers. They'd tormented them in grade school. The Palmers were born with a silver spoon in their mouths. Parker and Yukon went to school in hand-me-downs mended by their mother. They'd sworn never to work for them, and they'd gone without too many times to count even when the Palmers needed laborers.

Yukon was worth the sacrifice, even if Parker was only good enough for the most dangerous tasks and mucking out.

"You and Wade are my age, so tell me something," said Parker. "You okay living without a woman?"

Carlson narrowed his eyes. He began coiling a length of rope around his hand and elbow. "What's this all about? Is it something to do with Yukon and that girl from the diner?"

"It has to do with me. I'm forty-five. That's a lot of lonely years until I hang up my hat."

"Shit, you're depressing me," said Carlson. "I'm sure you'll find a woman when the time is right."

"I'm just not sure I can trust one again."

Carlson walked over to his truck and put the rope in the bed. He reached in his pocket for his keys. "How long you gonna live in the past? You fucked around with that girl, what, over twenty years ago? It's time to move on and expand your horizons, buddy."

Parker nodded.

"If you keep playing it safe, nothing will change. Sometimes you have to put yourself out there. I'm not saying there aren't any risks, and another bitch may break your heart, but eventually you'll find the right one."

Parker moved to the side as Carlson boarded his truck. "You're just like your dad. You have a way with words."

"I'll see you at Meg's tonight. You best be there." Carlson backed out of the driveway, disappearing down the drive.

His friend was right. He should have taken a risk and told Robyn he loved her.

Chapter Seventeen

A week later

Yukon brought his horse out of gallop and noticed someone standing near the barn. He walked his horse the rest of the way, giving her a breather. He'd been out scouting their distant property for any damage now that the ground had dried up enough to ride on.

As he neared his home, he saw that it was Robyn. It had been well over a week since she'd left. The hardest week of his life. Now she had the nerve to show up again?

A mix of anger, betrayal, and desire nearly knocked the breath out of him.

He dismounted his mare and tied her to the fence post. Yukon lifted his Stetson to fix his hair and set it back in place.

"Hi," she said.

"Can I help you?" He wanted to hate her, to tell her to fuck off, but he couldn't.

"I wanted to see you."

Yukon wasn't buying it. He made his way to the barn and grabbed the shovel, dropping it in a wheelbarrow. "I have nothing to say to you, Robyn."

"I'm sorry," she said. "Can't we please talk?"

He scoffed. "I'm taking a page from your playbook, darlin'. I refuse to deal with you or Parker anymore. I'm just worrying about myself from now on."

She rushed in front of him so he couldn't ignore her, pressing her palms to his chest. Damn, he missed her touch. Her hair smelled like strawberries.

"Don't be mad at your brother because of me. He loves you," she said.

"No, he's off riding in the rodeo every day after he swore he'd never ride again. I'm tired of people betraying me."

She shook her head. "He's not at the rodeo, Yukon. He's at the Palmer ranch."

He narrowed his eyes. "How would you know?"

"I saw him there last week when I was getting some contracts signed."

"He wouldn't be there. I know him. Maybe you saw someone else," he said, walking around her.

"Yukon, he was mucking out their stalls."

He squeezed his hands into fists, then turned around, his mind in a daze.

Mucking out? All these months he'd been pissed off at Parker, giving him the hardest time. The bastard had lowered himself to work for the Palmers just to keep food on their table? He hadn't been betraying Yukon, he'd been sacrificing for him.

"Why the fuck would he do that?" He was talking more to himself, frustration and anger surging out of nowhere.

"Because he loves you. No matter the cost."

"This can't be right. He told you this?"

"He didn't want to lose your respect."

Parker was a proud man, always had been. He believed in honor, family, and keeping his word. For him to stoop to beg the Palmers for work showed just how deep his loyalties to his family lied.

Where did that leave Robyn?

"What about you? You were real quick to run off, weren't you? Haven't heard from you since."

She looked down, kicking at the hay littering the floor of the barn. "I ran. You're right."

"Why? I thought there was something special between us. I actually started to believe we wanted the same things out of life."

This time she looked him in the eyes. "I'm not like you. I didn't have a great mom and dad growing up. Once I started having feelings for you, real feelings, it scared the hell out of me. I've always avoided getting close to people." She took a breath before continuing. "Because I'm scared."

"Of what?"

"I don't know." She spun around. "Maybe getting my heart broken, being tossed away when you get sick of me. I've lived a certain way my whole life, convincing myself of the kind of woman I should be. In reality, I'm not sure of anything … except you."

Yukon's bravado slipped away. He reached down for her hand, intertwining their fingers. "What are you saying?"

She swallowed hard, and she looked so helpless he had the urge to pull her into his arms. "I missed you. A lot. Can we give things a chance?"

"But you're heading back to the city soon."

"I've already gone back, Yukon. We left a few days ago. I thought things would go back to normal, that I'd be able to forget you. It wasn't so easy."

He walked back out to the yard between the house and the barn, still holding her hand. "So, whose car is that?"

Robyn chuckled. "It's mine. It barely got me here."

Yukon had been in a dark rut since Robyn left with barely a goodbye. He'd just gotten to know her, then she was gone. As much as he shouldn't trust her, seeing her again stripped away all the layers of sadness and depression. He wanted her in his life more than anything.

He spun around, conflicted on how he should

react. Yukon climbed the first rung of the paddock fence and sat on the top rail. "You telling me you drove all the way from the city to here by yourself? Because you missed me?"

"You have every right to hate me. I left when every instinct inside me told me to stay. I'm just so used to disappointment that the happiness terrified me."

"So, what now?" he asked.

Robyn walked over to the fence and braced a hand on each of his knees. "Were you telling me the truth when you said you wanted a future with me?"

"I had no reason to lie."

"What about now? Do you still feel the same way?" She slid both hands up his thighs, his cock reacting from the simple touch, hardening in his jeans.

He didn't answer.

She ran her palm over the bulge in his pants, then untucked the front of his shirt. "I missed this body," she said. When her roaming hands smoothed up his abs, he'd had enough.

Yukon shackled both her wrists in a hand and slipped off the fence. "What game are you playing? You have another assignment up here?"

Robyn tried to tug away, but he wouldn't let her. "I told you why I'm here. I made a mistake, probably the biggest mistake in my life. I've been looking for happiness in all the wrong places. I know that know."

He clenched his jaw, staring down at her beautiful face. Her long hair hung in loose curls over her shoulders and her lips were painted red. Yukon licked his lips as he looked lower. Her huge juicy tits were barely hidden in her tight black shirt. "You want me to trust you now? How do I know you won't run off again? I'm too old for this shit."

"Let me show you how serious I am." She licked

her lips, teasing and tempting him. He still hadn't released her wrists when Parker's truck came barreling up the long, winding drive. County music filled the quiet of the afternoon.

He'd been on bad terms with Parker since Robyn left, and now that he knew the truth about where he disappeared to every day, he felt like an asshole. Yukon still didn't need to hear Parker tell him "I told you so" and push Robyn away.

Robyn turned her head, and they both watched as Parker hopped down from his truck, fitting on his black Stetson before walking toward them.

"You're back," said Parker, circling them as he made a slow inspection of their runaway guest.

"Are you disappointed?" she asked.

"I never should have let you leave," said Parker.

****

Robyn was in a bind. Both the men who'd stolen her heart were there, and the idea of a ménage relationship could turn both of them off. She'd suggested it to Parker, but he never said anything one way or another.

After leaving for the city with Shelly and Peter, she swore she left her heart and soul behind in the country. She tried to focus on work, drinks at night, the same routine … but all she could think about were Parker, Yukon, and their simple life in paradise. It took her a few days of self-reflection to realize she'd been chasing rainbows her entire life. Trying to be something else just to be accepted by people she couldn't stand had stolen her zest for life. What she needed, what she'd always needed, was love, acceptance, and authenticity.

Parker looked like sin with his black Stetson, Wranglers, and fitted t-shirt hugging his hard muscles. His eyes were dark and set, making her body thrum. She still remembered their time in the barn loft—and driving away when the night was over, knowing she'd never see him again.

"I never should have left," she said. Robyn had never felt so vulnerable, her heart and life on the line. "I love both of you."

Yukon narrowed his eyes, but kept silent.

"And you still ran back to the city," said Parker. He approached her without apology, running the backs of his fingers along the swell of her breast. "You should be punished for putting my brother through a week of hell."

"You're right," she said. Out of everything, she felt the worst for hurting Yukon when he'd only been good to her. "I told Yukon about your job, too." It was supposed to be some big secret, but all this bad blood had to stop. She'd never had a real relative, and to see two brothers grow apart because of a misunderstanding was indigestible to her.

Parker and Yukon were silent.

"Why didn't you tell me?" asked Yukon. "All this time I thought you were breaking your promise."

Parker exhaled, pacing back and forth. "I did what I had to do. I'm not gonna apologize."

"Never asked you to," said Yukon. "You know how many times I considered going to the Palmers for work? The only reason I held back was because I knew you'd kill me."

"I would have," said Parker. "It's one thing for me to sink that low, another for my little brother."

She could feel their love like a living force all around them. Getting everything in the open was exactly what they needed.

"Neither of us needs to work for them. There's plenty of money to be made on our own land if we work together," said Yukon. "We'll get by."

"And what about her?" he said, jutting his chin toward her.

Both men assessed her. She swallowed and looked between them, wishing she knew what they were thinking. Her future was so uncertain. All her clothes were in the backseat of her car. She'd given notice to her landlord, and applied at a few jobs in the rodeo town she'd stayed in with Shelly. Robyn had taken a massive risk, inspired by Parker's tattoo. She needed to have courage and follow her heart.

"She needs a good spanking for messing with both of us," said Yukon.

"Robyn, get to my room," said Parker. "We all need to talk."

She listened to Parker, happy just to get back in the old house. At least they hadn't told her to fuck off after she'd screwed them both over. As soon as she passed the screen door, the scent of the brothers was like a comforting hug. The old, mismatched furniture that she used to turn her nose up to was a welcome sight. She'd changed her way of thinking so much since meeting the cowboys. Somehow, they managed to put her life in perspective where she'd failed for decades.

Robyn walked up the creaky steps, the brothers right on her heels.

"So when exactly did Parker tell you about the Palmer brothers?" asked Yukon.

"She paid me a visit before leaving for the city," said Parker. "We spent the night at the old barn."

Once they got in the room, the mood had shifted. Yukon crossed his arms, standing in the doorway. "You fucked her and didn't plan on mentioning that to me, either?"

Parker raised both arms to the sides. "She'd already left. I couldn't help myself. You're not the only one who fell for her."

Yukon shook his head. "No, you're the one who told me to stay away from her. Was that so you could take her for yourself?"

"Look, believe whatever the fuck you want." Parker made for the door, but she grabbed his arm before he could leave.

"Both of you, please, stop it. This is all my fault," she said. "I was confused, falling for two men, and trying to convince myself it could never work. I never planned on any of this. Never planned on putting a rift between the two of you, and I sure as hell never planned on falling in love."

Everyone got all quiet. She only wanted to feel their love. Shelly had told her she had completely lost her mind when she quit her job. She'd told Shelly she was moving back up to cattle country to live with the cowboy brothers. After laughing, then realizing Robyn wasn't playing around, she'd lost all respect for Robyn.

Calloway had replaced her within the hour, testament to her shitty life in the city. She was unneeded and unwanted, even after years of trying to fit in— dressing and acting the part counted for nothing.

"About that punishment." Yukon nodded to his brother.

"Okay, let's get this over with. Robyn, take off that skirt. Panties, too," said Parker.

Both men stood there, watching and waiting for her to comply. She was already hornier than hell just being around them. Robyn unzipped the back of her skirt and shimmied out of it. She hesitated before taking off her underwear. Parker shook his head, so she continued to slip out of them. He sat on the edge of his bed. The entire room smelled like his rich cologne.

"Over my lap," he said. "When we were young,

we'd get the belt from our father as punishment. You're lucky you just get my hand."

Oh boy. She approached him, and he immediately brought her forward over his lap. She wasn't sure what to expect, not ever certain if this was going to be painful or sexual. Robyn hoped the latter.

Once over his legs, he pulled her shirt higher so her entire ass was exposed. The air hit the moisture between her legs, and she hoped they couldn't see how aroused she was. Parker started rubbing soft circles over the globes of her ass. Her clit throbbed in anticipation.

"Such a beautiful, lush ass. Perfect for fucking." Parker brought his hand down hard on her ass, the fleshy sound echoing in the room.

"Ouch," she shouted.

"Look at that jiggle," said Yukon. "Do it again."

Parker spanked her two more times. The burn made her lust grow stronger. They were completely no holds barred. "There'll be no more running away." *Smack.* "No more lies." *Smack.* "You belong to us now." This time he kissed her reddened cheeks, then softly rubbed them. "Understand?"

"Yes," she said.

Parker moved his hand between her legs, impaling her with two fingers. She gasped, loving the feel of him being inside her in any way. When he dragged those fingers up toward her ass, she tensed. She knew what was coming, knew what would be involved with a ménage relationship, but it still scared her. Robyn had never experienced anal, or anything kinky for that matter.

Parker caressed her asshole with a finger, and she was surprised by the explosive sensations that scattered through her body. He pressed the tip of his finger in, and she clamped down hard.

"She's tighter than a fist. *A virgin.* Get the ginger root from the kitchen," said Parker. "She'll have to learn not to fight us."

Yukon left the bedroom, leaving them alone.

"Let me up," she said.

"Not yet, little lady. If you want both of us, we have to prepare you first. I don't know about men in the city, but cowboys have some tried and true ways to prepare a woman."

"For what?"

"You want two men. That means I'm going to claim this tight ass of yours. Yukon will fill your pussy at the same time. You'll be so full of cock, you'll know exactly where you belong."

The filthy image replayed over and over in her head. She was so close to an orgasm and they hadn't even started. She was relieved they were going along with the idea of a ménage that she didn't care what the fuck they did to her body.

Yukon was back soon after. She twisted her head and watched him use a pocket knife to whittle a big piece of ginger root. What the fuck was that for? She had no clue what these cowboys were up to, but she hoped they wouldn't hurt her.

"What's that for, Yukon?"

"It'll make things easier when we double-fuck you. You'll get a bit numb, get used to being stretched, and learn not to clamp down."

He squatted down in front on her holding the carved root and a tube of clear lubricant. She was still vulnerably stretched over Parker's lap. The root was shaped like some kind of butt plug. He drizzled lubricant all over it, then passed the container to Parker.

She jolted when the cool, slippery substance was poured over her asshole. "Relax," said Parker. "Relaxing is key here. You'll learn that soon." He massaged the lubricant over her virgin hole, then began to insert a finger. She tensed again, but he tutted.

Yukon was still near her head, stroking her hair. "Relax for Parker. He won't hurt you."

Robyn stopped tightening and accepted Parker's big finger. The foreign feeling was oddly titillating, the sensations reaching all the way to her clit. Once he'd filled her, he added a second finger. Her breathing picked up with her nerves.

"I can't do this," she said.

"You're doing great, darlin'," said Yukon. "Almost there."

She bit the inside of her cheek as Parker slowly scissored his fingers, stretching her ass. Then Yukon passed him the ginger, and he replaced his fingers with the hard, slick root. He pushed it in until it lodged into place, holding her ass open.

"There we go," said Parker. "Now, don't clamp down, no matter what, or it'll burn like a bitch. Understand?"

She nodded. As soon as she consented, they helped her to her feet. It felt weird with the root stuck inside her ass. She stood awkwardly, holding onto Yukon's arm for balance.

"What are you doing to me?"

"You'll be glad we prepared you properly," said Yukon. "We're not small men."

She could attest to that fact. They had the biggest cocks she'd ever seen.

They undressed her all the way until she was completely nude. Yukon bent down and supported one of her tits, taking her nipple in his mouth. Parker pressed his body against her from behind, reaching to cup her pussy. He played with her clit and the moment she clenched, the ginger burned the tender tissues in her ass.

Robyn squealed.

"You have to relax, baby. Accept the pleasure. Don't fight it," Parker whispered against her neck. He tongued the shell of her ear, teasing her erogenous zone until she closed her eyes. The dual assault on her body had her spiraling out of control. It was so good, so intense, their mouths and hands everywhere.

This was better than she imagined, and she had a vivid imagination.

After the delicious foreplay seemed to carry on forever, they stopped. "I think she's ready," said Yukon. Robyn was already in a half-daze, savoring the sensations, not thinking about anything but here and now.

Yukon kicked off his jeans and boxers and sat on his brother's queen bed, his rock-hard erection pointing up like a virile arrow.

Yukon leaned back on his elbows, reaching one hand forward to hold the base of his cock.

Parker led her forward. "Straddle Yukon, baby. Sit on his cock."

She was panting now, so eager to be fucked it was obscene. Robyn crawled over him until she straddled his hips.

"Good girl. Come on, sweetheart. I want to feel your hot little cunt. Give me what's mine." Yukon helped her impale herself on his thick cock. She was so wet from arousal, easily sinking down on his length. Yukon groaned as he filled her, and she moaned, loving the fullness. The root began to burn from the pressure, but Parker was quick to remove it. She heard it drop to the floor.

"Get ready to take another man, Robyn. Just relax and push back against me." Parker's cockhead waited at her forbidden hole, demanding entrance. She was already stretched and the root left a numbing effect, so there was no pain as he worked his dick past her anal ring. Her body felt like it would explode as the two cocks fought to fit inside her body at the same time. She was so full, so thoroughly claimed.

Once Parker was seated to the hilt, his entire dick deep in her asshole, he froze, not moving a muscle. He cooed, running the tips of his fingers up and down her bare back until she was relaxed and calm.

"Hurry up, Parker. I'm dying here," said Yukon.

"Man up. We need to take our time with her." Parker began to ever so slowly pull his cock out, then in, then out again. He picked up the rhythm, and Yukon joined him. They pistoned in and out of her like a machine, in perfect sync the entire time.

"Oh fuck, you're tight, baby girl." Parker held her hips in a bruising grip as he stood behind her, pummeling her ass. Yukon suckled her tits as he fucked her from underneath. It was so good, more than she could have hoped for.

The overload of pleasure brought the promise of an orgasm to remember. "I'm close. Oh God, I'm going to come hard."

"Let it all go, baby. Come all over our cocks," said Yukon. He kissed her on the mouth, silencing her cries as the orgasm finally splintered inside of her. She broke from the kiss, panting and crying out as colored light passed behind her closed eyes. Her release went on and on, her pussy and ass throbbing and squeezing the brothers until they joined her.

Parker was first, filling her ass before gently slipping out. Yukon followed, holding her hips as he pumped into her from beneath, her entire body quivering.

She collapsed over him after he came inside her,

his sweat-slick body hot against her breasts.

"That was perfect," said Parker. She heard the tap in the bathroom next to his bedroom. He came back in and asked her to spread her legs. With gentle strokes, he cleansed the cum from her legs, and wiped her clean. Her body was still a hotwire and she gasped each time he rubbed a sensitive spot.

He climbed on his bed, and she fell asleep between them, feeling safe, wanted, and home.

Epilogue

Eight months later

"They're so cute," Robyn said. The tiny yellow chicks were chirping up a storm as Parker and Yukon brought in plastic crates full of sexed future hens, stacking them inside the new barn.

"Don't get too attached. They're not pets," said Parker.

"They'll be egg layers, so I don't see a problem with getting to know them." Robyn rubbed her rounded stomach as she watched her men busy at work. They were getting started in their new venture, an egg farm. There were already so many cattle farms in the area, and the crops weren't enough to survive on, so they decided to go into eggs. Organic eggs. Robyn knew the demand for organic food in the cities, and after using her connections, and putting her business degree to good use, they started their own farm. They had some start-up loans, but things looked very promising for their family farm.

The brothers worked well together, the perfect team. They had hope and didn't have to worry about dying alone. Both of them continually told her she'd saved them. In reality, they'd saved her.

Yukon took off his Stetson and rubbed his sleeve against his forehead. "How're my babies?" he asked.

"We're doing good. You guys should take a break. You've been at it for hours," she said. Robyn was six months pregnant. She never imagined herself a mother, especially at her age, but she was excited. It was her chance to make things right, to break the cycle and be a great mom to her baby. She'd make sure it was always loved, wanted, and had everything it needed. They didn't know who fathered the baby out of the two of them—it didn't matter. They were a family.

Parker and Yukon each took one of Robyn's hands. They left their barn and walked to the fence line that looked out into the freshly planted fields.

"Looks like it'll be a good harvest this year," said Parker. "The weather's been better than last year, that's for sure."

"Everything's looking up," said Yukon. His blue eyes appeared to sparkle in the sunlight. "I can't wait to teach our baby everything about farming." He rubbed her belly and kissed her temple.

"We have something for you," said Parker. He dug in his pocket and pulled out a ring. It was the same ring she'd found in the shoebox at the top of his closet. "This was our mother's ring, Robyn. It's all we have left of her besides some pictures. We want you to have it. You're our woman now, the mother of our child, and we'll take care of you both for the rest of our lives."

He put the ring on her finger, then kissed her hand. Yukon watched, and she saw his eyes glisten. Their mother meant a lot to them.

The spring breeze was getting warmer, bringing notes for fresh-turned earth through the air. Robyn kissed both cowboys. Her love for them grew more each day, and she never regretted the decision to take the risk and give up everything for love.

"She traded her briefcase for an egg basket, Parker. Literally. And you said it would never happen," Yukon teased. They all laughed as they reminisced. So much had happened in the last year, and she was excited for what was to come.

Shelly said Prince Charming didn't exist, that

happily ever afters weren't realistic. Robyn knew better. She'd just been looking in all the wrong places.

The End

www.staceyespino.com

STACEY ESPINO

EVERNIGHT PUBLISHING ®

www.evernightpublishing.com